The Touchstone

Edith Wharton

ET REMOTISSIMA PROPE

100 PAGES

100 PAGES

Published by Hesperus Press Limited
4 Rickett Street, London SW6 1RU
www.hesperuspress.com

First published in *Scribner's Magazine* in 1900
This edition first published by Hesperus Press Limited, 2003

The Touchstone © Edith Wharton, 1900
Foreword © Salley Vickers, 2003

Designed and typeset by Fraser Muggeridge
Printed in the United Arab Emirates by Oriental Press

ISBN: 1-84391-066-7

CONTENTS

FOREWORD

Edith Wharton's reputation stands in the shade of her more famous male contemporary and friend, Henry James, as a graceful larch might to a venerable yew. All intimacies involve a degree of reciprocity, and without question the two novelists informed and influenced each other's work, not simply with respect to subject matter and outlook but also to style: the famously – or notoriously, according to your preferences – complex parenthetical rhythms of James resonate, if less taxingly, in the decorous prose of Edith Wharton, just as her colleague's scrutinising focus on the discreet dance of consciousness and human interconnectedness echoes in her subtle themes.

Both Wharton and James were fascinated by the lurking, misty dangers that inevitably accompany the exercise of free will; in the diabolical traps we set ourselves through self-referential obtuseness and self-protective blindness. No theme is more compelling to either novelist than the human tendency to squander true freedom – the freedom of conscience or the unsullied soul – in the pursuit of the, seemingly wider, scope and vistas in which to play out fantasies of self-fulfilment. Any act of choice involves a necessary limitation, and the aetiology of moral choice, and its attendant unforeseen consequences, forms the root of high drama in the works of both novelists.

The Touchstone, first published in 1900, is a taut novella with reverberations of two of James's finest late novels, *The Wings of the Dove* and *The Golden Bowl*. Both the better-known novels and the novella examine the ways in which love, however authentic, can be vitiated through the violation of another's affection and trust. Glennard is a struggling lawyer who cannot afford to marry his heart's choice, Alexa Trent, who is in the luckless position – like so many accomplished and financially constrained women of the time – of being the unpaid companion to a rich aunt. Through an advertisement in a paper, Glennard becomes aware that his singular, and intimate, correspondence with a dead woman novelist is capable of providing him with the money necessary for them to marry. He had known the intellectually brilliant Mrs Aubyn in his youth, and what amounts to her developing infatuation with him is unambiguously recorded in her stream of letters:

> 'Her letters! Why, he must have hundreds of them – enough to fill a volume. Sometimes it used to seem to him that they came with every post – he used to avoid looking in his letter-box when he came home to his rooms – her writing seemed to spring out at him as he put his key in the door.'

The passage illustrates a tone which is borrowed from no one, but is supremely Wharton's own. A dry and energetic humour is inherent in that 'spring' – yet it is more than simply funny; it is also penetrating, for from it we apprehend something potentially tragic in Glennard (even, perhaps, in Wharton's view, something inherently tragic in the masculine make-up): a fragility that stems from a fearfulness of emotional intensity.

Mrs Aubyn, the generator of this fearfulness, does not escape the sharply humorous observations of her creator:

> 'all her clothes had an impersonal air, as though they had belonged to someone else and been borrowed in an emergency that had somehow become chronic. She was conscious enough of her deficiencies to try to amend them by rash imitations of the most approved models; but no woman who does not dress well intuitively will ever do so

by the light of reason, and Mrs Aubyn's plagiarisms, to borrow a metaphor of her trade, somehow never seemed to be incorporated with the text.'

The tone is more Jane Austen, at her least socially indulgent, than Henry James, but it is given a further twist in the reflexive use of the metaphor drawn from the very art that Wharton is mistress of. Mrs Aubyn is a novelist and a woman of remarkable intellectual attainment: a 'woman of genius with her long pale face and short-sighted eyes'. It seems, to me, entirely possible that the model for the physically uninspiring but mentally stimulating Mrs Aubyn was George Eliot, to whom there is a fleeting reference in Chapter 4, and who was also deceased by the time *The Touchstone* was written, but whose reputation for being a savante as well as a novelist was then enjoying full acclaim. If this surmise is correct there is possibly some personal animosity at work: remarks such as 'genius is of small use to a woman who does not know how to do her hair' are clearly Wharton's own tart voice and not her protagonist, Glennard's. Henry James, with uncharacteristic deadpan chivalry, once declared himself 'in love' with the horse-faced Marian Evans, and to a woman of Edith Wharton's refinement it might well have rankled that it was the physically unprepossessing and, in literary terms, more highly regarded novelist who gained the hold on so many men, never mind one who was Wharton's special confidant and friend.

However, if there was some grit of personal experience in the portrait of Mrs Aubyn, Wharton was artist enough to work any coruscating jealousy into service in the alchemy of her tale. Indeed, 'alchemy' is a pertinent term in a story which has much to do with baseness and gold, and the mutable connection between the two in the human psyche.

The friendship between Mrs Aubyn and Glennard enacts for us that uneasy disjunction in any relationship where affection is not equally matched and which thus always threatens to dissolve, on one side, into an atypical brutality and, on the other, into a faintly accusing masochism. The fatal ambivalence on Glennard's side is brilliantly done. 'He was tired of her already – he was always tired of her – yet he was not sure he wanted her to go.' Such insights into the essential paradox of human motivation are part of Wharton's particular genius. 'It was one of the laws of Glennard's intercourse with Miss Trent that he always went to see her the day after he had resolved to give her up.'

There is a miasma of unease which is generated throughout this story: the word 'irritation' appears no less than seven times, and for a writer as fastidious as Wharton this can be no accident. Irritation is the scourge of the sensitive, and Glennard has that type of sensitivity which hovers between rank egotism and moral good taste. Part of the function of the word is to signal his own apprehension of potential disaster in the steps he takes in betraying the woman who loved him in order to capture the woman he himself loves. To sell the unique collection of letters he employs the services of Flamel, a collector of books and a man, in Glennard's own view, of equivocal character. 'Flamel hesitated; and almost immediately Glennard's scruples gave way to irritation. If at this hour Flamel were to affect an inopportune reluctance –!'

Ironically, it is Flamel who proves, in the event, the more morally admirable. Unaware that Glennard is any more than the legal custodian of the letters, he undertakes their sale, and the published volumes become a talking point and sensation: so much so that Glennard is unable to prevent the woman whom the publication has empowered him to marry from sharing in the widespread feeling that the anonymous recipient of the Aubyn letters has acted despicably. Again, Wharton demonstrates her psychological acumen, as, lacking any other confidant, Glennard draws closer to the man who has aided him while becoming more and more convinced – an inevitable consequence of his own treachery – that, in order to advance the cause of his own affections, Flamel has, in turn, betrayed Glennard to his wife, not only by revealing his role in the publication, but by confiding to her the true identity of the man to whom the letters were addressed.

'Glennard burst into a coarse laugh. "How much longer do you expect me to keep up that pretence about the letters? You knew well enough they were written to me."

Flamel looked at him in silence. "Were they?" he said at length. "I didn't know it."

"And didn't suspect it, I suppose," Glennard sneered.

The other was again silent; then he said, "I may remind you that, supposing I had felt any curiosity about the matter, I had no way of finding out that the letters were written to you. You never showed me the originals."

"What does that prove? There were fifty ways of finding out. It's the kind of thing one can easily do."

Flamel glanced at him with contempt. "Our ideas probably differ as to what a man can easily do." '

As Wharton dryly comments: 'We live in our own souls as in an unmapped region…' Not only does Glennard disastrously lose his own sense of integrity and make the humiliating discovery that he is a lesser man than the one he has used and despised, but he also loses the love he has for the wife for whom he has undertaken this Faustian transaction. In a desperate attempt to forestall the worst effects of Flamel's supposed treachery, and to relieve himself of the intolerable burden of secrecy, Glennard arranges for his wife to 'discover' his role in the publication of the *Aubyn Letters*, and his next dire punishment is to learn that he cannot bear that she should be aware of his turpitude yet make no apparent protest over it. Projecting all his guilt onto her, he is left beached up on the shore of a self-engendered and loveless isolation. 'Every other passion, he mused, left some mark upon the nature; but love passed like the flight of a ship across the waters.'

Perversely, remorse summons what passion and constancy failed to achieve, and he comes to feel for the dead woman whose memory he has so shabbily exploited:

> 'The shame was deep, but it was a renovating anguish; he was like a man whom intolerable pain has roused from the creeping lethargy of death...
>
> He rose next morning to as fresh a sense of life as though his hour of mute communion with Margaret Aubyn had been a more exquisite renewal of their earlier meetings... he felt an intense fear of losing the sense of her nearness.'

'Only the fact that we are unaware how well our nearest know us enables us to live with them.' The finely phrased 'renovating anguish' serves its turn for, in no soft-soap sense, this is a genuine story of redemption. Glennard's reticent wife, Alexa, loves him and therefore sees deeply enough to have surmised what he has done and, in deference to her keen sense of his suffering, has kept the knowledge tacit between them. But she also has the sensibility to comprehend the other woman's love, and to recognise that what has occurred is, ultimately, beneficent. It is Alexa who frees Glennard into the knowledge of the full outcome of his actions which requires more of him than the luxury of self-abasement; for, through recognition of his own perfidy, he has grown in moral strength and character and has become, finally, worthy of the love of the woman he has had to betray in order to grow sufficiently in stature to receive the rewards of expanded consciousness. The original UK published title was *The Gift from the Grave*, and the equivocal but ultimately triumphant ending is a chilling testament to the power of love to extend beyond mere corporeal existence, to educate and enlighten, and, painfully, to transform.

– Salley Vickers, 2003

The Touchstone

Professor Joslin, who, as our readers are doubtless aware, is engaged in writing the life of Mrs Aubyn, asks us to state that he will be greatly indebted to any of the famous novelist's friends who will furnish him with information concerning the period previous to her coming to England. Mrs Aubyn had so few intimate friends, and consequently so few regular correspondents, that letters will be of special value. Professor Joslin's address is 10 Augusta Gardens, Kensington, and he begs us to say that he will promptly return any documents entrusted to him.

Glennard dropped the *Spectator* and sat looking into the fire. The club was filling up, but he still had to himself the small inner room with its darkening outlook down the rain-streaked prospect of Fifth Avenue. It was all dull and dismal enough, yet a moment earlier his boredom had been perversely tinged by a sense of resentment at the thought that, as things were going, he might in time have to surrender even the despised privilege of boring himself within those particular four walls. It was not that he cared much for the club, but that the remote contingency of having to give it up stood to him, just then, perhaps by very reason of its insignificance and remoteness, for the symbol of his increasing abnegations; of that perpetual paring-off that was gradually reducing existence to the naked business of keeping himself alive. It was the futility of his multiplied shifts and privations that made them seem unworthy of a high attitude – the sense that, however rapidly he eliminated the superfluous, his cleared horizon was likely to offer no nearer view of the one prospect toward which he strained. To give up things in order to marry the woman one loves is easier than to give them up without being brought appreciably nearer to such a conclusion.

Through the open door he saw young Hollingsworth rise with a yawn from the ineffectual solace of a brandy-and-soda and transport his purposeless person to the window. Glennard measured his course with a contemptuous eye. It was so like Hollingsworth to get up and look out of the window just as it was growing too dark to see anything! There was a man rich enough to do what he pleased – had he been capable of being pleased – yet barred from all conceivable achievement by his own impervious dullness; while, a few feet off, Glennard, who wanted only enough to keep a decent coat on his back and a roof over the head of the woman he loved – Glennard, who had sweated, toiled, denied himself for the scant measure of opportunity that his zeal would have converted into a kingdom – sat wretchedly calculating that, even when he had resigned from the club, and knocked off his cigars, and given up his Sundays out of town, he would still be no nearer to attainment.

The *Spectator* had slipped to his feet, and as he picked it up his eye fell again on the paragraph addressed to the friends of Mrs Aubyn. He had read it for the first time with a scarcely perceptible quickening of attention: her name had so long been public property that his eye passed it unseeingly, as the crowd in the street hurries without a glance by some familiar monument.

Information concerning the period previous to her coming to England... The words were an evocation. He saw her again as she had looked at their first meeting, the poor woman of genius with her long pale face and short-sighted eyes, softened a little by the grace of youth and inexperience, but so incapable even then of any hold upon the pulses. When she spoke, indeed, she was wonderful, more wonderful, perhaps, than when later, to Glennard's fancy at least, the conscious-ness of memorable things uttered seemed to take from even her most intimate speech the perfect bloom of privacy. It was in those earliest days, if ever, that he had come near loving her; though even then his sentiment had lived only in the intervals of its expression. Later, when to be loved by her had been a state to touch any man's imagination, the physical reluctance had, inexplicably, so overborne the intellectual attraction, that the last years had been, to both of them, an agony of conflicting impulses. Even now, if, in turning over old papers, his hand lit on her letters, the touch filled him with inarticulate misery…

She had so few intimate friends… that letters will be of special value. So few intimate friends! For years she had had but one; one who in the last years had requited her wonderful pages, her tragic outpourings of love, humility, and pardon, with the scant phrases by which a man evades the vulgarest of sentimental importunities. He had been a brute in spite of himself, and sometimes, now that the remembrance of her face had faded, and only her voice and words remained with him, he chafed at his own inadequacy, his stupid inability to rise to the height of her passion. His egoism was not of a kind to mirror its complacency in the adventure. To have been loved by the most brilliant woman of her day, and to have been incapable of loving her, seemed to him, in looking back, derisive evidence of his limitations; and his remorseful tenderness for her memory was complicated with a sense of irritation against her for having given him once for all the measure of his emotional capacity. It was not often, however, that he thus probed the past. The public, in taking possession of Mrs Aubyn, had eased his shoulders of their burden. There was something fatuous in an attitude of sentimental apology towards a memory already classic: to reproach one's self for not having loved Margaret Aubyn was a good deal like being disturbed by an inability to admire the Venus of Milo. From her cold niche of fame she looked down ironically enough on his self-flagellations... It was only when he came on something that belonged to her that he felt a sudden renewal of the old feeling, the strange dual impulse that drew him to her voice but drove him from her hand, so that even now, at sight of anything she had touched, his heart contracted painfully. It happened seldom nowadays. Her little presents, one by one, had disappeared from his rooms, and her letters, kept from some unacknowledged puerile vanity in the possession of such treasures, seldom came beneath his hand...

Her letters will be of special value – Her letters! Why, he must have hundreds of them – enough to fill a volume. Sometimes it used to seem to him that they came with every post – he used to avoid looking in his letter-box when he came home to his rooms – but her writing seemed to spring out at him as he put his key in the door.

He stood up and strolled into the other room. Hollingsworth, lounging away from the window, had joined himself to a languidly convivial group of men, to whom, in phrases as halting as though they struggled to define an ultimate idea, he was expounding the cursed nuisance of living in a hole with such a damned climate that one had to get out of it by February, with the contingent difficulty of there being no place to take one's yacht to in winter but that other played-out hole, the Riviera. From the outskirts of this group Glennard wandered to another, where a voice as different as possible from Hollingsworth's colourless organ dominated another circle of languid listeners.

'Come and hear Dinslow talk about his patent: admission free,' one of the men sang out in a tone of mock resignation.

Dinslow turned to Glennard the confident pugnacity of his smile. 'Give it another six months and it'll be talking about itself,' he declared. 'It's pretty nearly articulate now.'

'Can it say papa?' someone else enquired.

Dinslow's smile broadened. 'You'll be deuced glad to say papa to *it* a year from now,' he retorted. 'It'll be able to support even you in affluence. Look here, now, just let me explain to you –'

Glennard moved away impatiently. The men at the club – all but those who were 'in it' – were proverbially 'tired' of Dinslow's patent, and none more so than Glennard, whose knowledge of its merits made it loom large in the depressing catalogue of lost opportunities. The relations between the two men had always been friendly, and Dinslow's urgent offers to 'take him in on the ground floor' had of late intensified Glennard's sense of his own inability to meet good luck halfway. Some of the men who had paused to listen were already in evening clothes, others on their way home to dress; and Glennard, with an accustomed twinge of humiliation, said to himself that if he lingered among them it was in the miserable hope that one of the number might ask him to dine. Miss Trent had told him that she was to go to the opera that evening with her rich aunt; and if he should have the luck to pick up a dinner invitation he might join her there without extra outlay.

He moved about the room, lingering here and there in a tentative affectation of interest; but though the men greeted him pleasantly, no one asked him to dine. Doubtless they were all engaged, these men who could afford to pay for their dinners, who did not have to hunt for invitations as a beggar rummages for a crust in an ash-barrel! But no – as Hollingsworth left the lessening circle about the table, an admiring youth called out, 'Holly, stop and dine!'

Hollingsworth turned on him the crude countenance that looked like the wrong side of a more finished face. 'Sorry I can't. I'm in for a beastly banquet.'

Glennard threw himself into an armchair. Why go home in the rain to dress? It was folly to take a cab to the opera, it was worse folly to go there at all. His perpetual meetings with Alexa Trent were as unfair to the girl as they were unnerving to himself. Since he couldn't marry her, it was time to stand aside and give a better man the chance – and his thought admitted the ironical implication that in the terms of expediency the phrase might stand for Hollingsworth.

2

He dined alone and walked home to his rooms in the rain. As he turned into Fifth Avenue he caught the wet gleam of carriages on their way to the opera, and he took the first side street, in a moment of irritation against the petty restrictions that thwarted every impulse. It was ridiculous to give up the opera, not because one might possibly be bored there, but because one must pay for the experiment.

In his sitting room, the tacit connivance of the inanimate had centred the lamplight on a photograph of Alexa Trent, placed, in the obligatory silver frame, just where, as memory officiously reminded him, Margaret Aubyn's picture had long throned in its stead. Miss Trent's features cruelly justified the usurpation. She had the kind of beauty that comes of a happy accord of face and spirit. It is not given to many to have the lips and eyes of their rarest mood, and some women go through life behind a mask expressing only their anxiety about the butcher's bill or their inability to see a joke. With Miss Trent, face and mind had the same high serious contour. She looked like a throned Justice by some grave Florentine painter; and it seemed to Glennard that her most salient attribute, or that at least to which her conduct gave most consistent expression, was a kind of passionate justness – the intuitive feminine justness that is so much rarer than a reasoned impartiality. Circumstances had tragically combined to develop this instinct into a conscious habit. She had seen more than most girls of the shabby side of life, of the perpetual tendency of want to cramp the noblest attitude. Poverty and misfortune had overhung her childhood, and she had none of the pretty delusions about life that are supposed to be the crowning grace of girlhood. This very competence, which gave her a touching reasonableness, made Glennard's situation more difficult than if he had aspired to a princess bred in the purple. Between them they asked so little – they knew so well how to make that little do – but they understood also, and she especially did not for a moment let him forget, that without that little the future they dreamed of was impossible.

The sight of her photograph quickened Glennard's exasperation. He was sick and ashamed of the part he was playing. He had loved her now for two years, with the tranquil tenderness that gathers depth and volume as it nears fulfilment; he knew that she would wait for him – but the certitude was an added pang. There are times when the constancy of the woman one cannot marry is almost as trying as that of the woman one does not want to.

Glennard turned up his reading lamp and stirred the fire. He had a long evening before him, and he wanted to crowd out thought with action. He had brought some papers from his office and he spread them out on his table and squared himself to the task...

It must have been an hour later that he found himself automatically fitting a key into a locked drawer. He had no more notion than a somnambulist of the mental process that had led up to this action. He was just dimly aware of having pushed aside the papers and the heavy calf volumes that a moment before had bounded his horizon, and of laying in their place, without a trace of conscious volition, the parcel he had taken from the drawer.

The letters were tied in packets of thirty or forty. There were a great many packets. On some of the envelopes the ink was fading; on others, which bore the English postmark, it was still fresh. She had been dead hardly three years, and she had written, at lengthening intervals, to the last...

He undid one of the early packets – little notes written during their first acquaintance at Hillbridge. Glennard, on leaving college, had begun life in his uncle's law office in the old university town. It was there that, at the house of her father, Professor Forth, he had first met the young lady then chiefly distinguished for having, after two years of a conspicuously unhappy marriage, returned to the protection of the paternal roof.

Mrs Aubyn was at that time an eager and somewhat tragic young woman, of complex mind and undeveloped manners, whom her crude experience of matrimony had fitted out with a stock of generalisations that exploded like bombs in the academic air of Hillbridge. In her choice of a husband she had been fortunate enough, if the paradox be permitted, to light on one so signally gifted with the faculty of putting himself in the wrong that her leaving him had the dignity of a manifesto –

made her, as it were, the spokeswoman of outraged wifehood. In this light she was cherished by that dominant portion of Hillbridge society which was least indulgent to conjugal differences, and which found a proportionate pleasure in being for once able to feast openly on a dish liberally seasoned with the outrageous. So much did this endear Mrs Aubyn to the university ladies, that they were disposed from the first to allow her more latitude of speech and action than the ill-used wife was generally accorded in Hillbridge, where misfortune was still regarded as a visitation designed to put people in their proper place and make them feel the superiority of their neighbours. The young woman so privileged combined with a kind of personal shyness an intellectual audacity that was like a deflected impulse of coquetry: one felt that if she had been prettier she would have had emotions instead of ideas. She was in fact even then what she had always remained: a genius capable of the acutest generalisations, but curiously undiscerning where her personal susceptibilities were concerned. Her psychology failed her just where it serves most women, and one felt that her brains would never be a guide to her heart. Of all this, however, Glennard thought little in the first year of their acquaintance. He was at an age when all the gifts and graces are but so much undiscriminated food to the ravening egoism of youth. In seeking Mrs Aubyn's company he was prompted by an intuitive taste for the best as a pledge of his own superiority. The sympathy of the cleverest woman in Hillbridge was balm to his craving for distinction; it was public confirmation of his secret sense that he was cut out for a bigger place. It must not be understood that Glennard was vain. Vanity contents itself with the coarsest diet; there is no palate so fastidious as that of self-distrust. To a youth of Glennard's aspirations the encouragement of a clever woman stood for the symbol of all success. Later, when he had begun to feel his way, to gain a foothold, he would not need such support; but it served to carry him lightly and easily over what is often a period of insecurity and discouragement.

It would be unjust, however, to represent his interest in Mrs Aubyn as a matter of calculation. It was as instinctive as love, and it missed being love by just such a hair's breadth deflection from the line of beauty as had determined the curve of Mrs Aubyn's lips. When they met she had just published her first novel, and Glennard, who afterwards had an ambitious man's impatience of distinguished women, was young enough to be dazzled by the semi-publicity it gave her. It was the kind of book that makes elderly ladies lower their voices and call each other 'my dear' when they furtively discuss it; and Glennard exulted in the superior knowledge of the world that enabled him to take as a matter of course sentiments over which the university shook its head. Still more delightful was it to hear Mrs Aubyn waken the echoes of academic drawing rooms with audacities surpassing those of her printed page. Her intellectual independence gave a touch of comradeship to their intimacy, prolonging the illusion of college friendships based on a joyous interchange of heresies. Mrs Aubyn and Glennard represented to each other the augur's wink behind the Hillbridge idol: they walked together in that light of young omniscience from which fate so curiously excludes one's elders.

Husbands who are notoriously inopportune may even die inopportunely, and this was the revenge that Mr Aubyn, some two years after her return to Hillbridge, took upon his injured wife. He died precisely at the moment when Glennard was beginning to criticise her. It was not that she bored him; she did what was infinitely worse – she made him feel his inferiority. The sense of mental equality had been gratifying to his raw ambition; but as his self-knowledge defined itself, his understanding of her also increased; and if man is at times indirectly flattered by the moral superiority of woman, her mental ascendancy is extenuated by no such oblique tribute to his powers. The attitude of looking up is a strain on the muscles; and it was becoming more and more Glennard's opinion that brains, in a woman, should be merely the obverse of beauty. To beauty Mrs Aubyn could lay no claim; and while she had enough prettiness to exasperate him by her incapacity to make use of it, she seemed invincibly ignorant of any of the little artifices whereby women contrive to hide their defects and even to turn them into graces. Her dress never seemed a part of her; all her clothes had an impersonal air, as though they had belonged to someone else and been borrowed in an emergency that had somehow become chronic. She was conscious enough of her deficiencies to try to amend them by rash imitations of the most approved models; but no woman who does not dress well intuitively will ever do so by the light of reason, and Mrs Aubyn's plagiarisms, to borrow a metaphor of her trade, somehow never seemed to be incorporated with the text.

Genius is of small use to a woman who does not know how to do her hair. The fame that came to Mrs Aubyn with her second book left Glennard's imagination untouched, or had at most the negative effect of removing her still further from the circle of his contracting sympathies. We are all the sport of time; and fate had so perversely ordered the chronology of Margaret Aubyn's romance that when her husband died Glennard felt as though he had lost a friend.

It was not in his nature to be needlessly unkind; and though he was in the impregnable position of the man who has given a woman no more definable claim on him than that of letting her fancy that he loves her, he would not for the world have accentuated his advantage by any betrayal of indifference. During the first year of her widowhood their friendship dragged on with halting renewals of sentiment, becoming more and more a banquet of empty dishes from which the covers were never removed; then Glennard went to New York to live and exchanged the faded pleasures of intercourse for the comparative novelty of correspondence. Her letters, oddly enough, seemed at first to bring her nearer than her presence. She had adopted, and she successfully maintained, a note as affectionately impersonal as his own; she wrote ardently of her work, she questioned him about his, she even bantered him on the inevitable pretty girl who was certain before long to divert the current of his confidences. To Glennard, who was almost a stranger in New York, the sight of Mrs Aubyn's writing was like a voice of reassurance in surroundings as yet insufficiently aware of him. His vanity found a retrospective enjoyment in the sentiment his heart had rejected, and this factitious emotion drove him once or twice to Hillbridge, whence, after scenes of evasive tenderness, he returned dissatisfied with himself and her. As he made room for himself in New York and peopled the space he had cleared with the sympathies at the disposal of agreeable and self-confident young men, it seemed to him natural to infer that Mrs Aubyn had refurnished in the same manner the void he was not unwilling his departure should have left. But in the dissolution of sentimental partnerships it is seldom that both associates are able to withdraw their funds at the same time; and Glennard gradually learned that he stood for the venture on which Mrs Aubyn had irretrievably staked her all. It was not the kind of figure he cared to cut. He had no fancy for leaving havoc in

14

his wake and would have preferred to sow a quick growth of oblivion in the spaces wasted by his unconsidered inroads; but if he supplied the seed, it was clearly Mrs Aubyn's business to see to the raising of the crop. Her attitude seemed indeed to throw his own reasonableness into distincter relief; so that they might have stood for thrift and improvidence in an allegory of the affections.

It was not that Mrs Aubyn permitted herself to be a pensioner on his bounty. He knew she had no wish to keep herself alive on the small change of sentiment; she simply fed on her own funded passion, and the luxuries it allowed her made him, even then, dimly aware that she had the secret of an inexhaustible alchemy.

Their relations remained thus negatively tender till she suddenly wrote him of her decision to go abroad to live. Her father had died, she had no near ties in Hillbridge, and London offered more scope than New York to her expanding personality. She was already famous, and her laurels were yet unharvested.

For a moment the news roused Glennard to a jealous sense of lost opportunities. He wanted, at any rate, to reassert his power before she made the final effort of escape. They had not met for over a year, but of course he could not let her sail without seeing her. She came to New York the day before her departure, and they spent its last hours together. Glennard had planned no course of action – he simply meant to let himself drift. They both drifted, for a long time, down the languid current of reminiscence; she seemed to sit passive, letting him push his way back through the overgrown channels of the past. At length she reminded him that they must bring their explorations to an end. He rose to leave, and stood looking at her with the same uncertainty in his heart. He was tired of her already – he was always tired of her – yet he was not sure that he wanted her to go.

'I may never see you again,' he said, as though confidently appealing to her compassion.

Her look enveloped him. 'And I shall see you always – always!'

'Why go then –?' escaped him.

'To be nearer you,' she answered; and the words dismissed him like a closing door.

The door was never to reopen; but through its narrow crack Glennard, as the years went on, became more and more conscious of an inextinguishable light directing its small ray towards the past which consumed so little of his own commemorative oil. The reproach was taken from this thought by Mrs Aubyn's gradual translation into terms of universality. In becoming a personage she so naturally ceased to be a person that Glennard could almost look back to his explorations of her spirit as on a visit to some famous shrine, immortalised, but in a sense desecrated, by popular veneration.

Her letters from London continued to come with the same tender punctuality; but the altered conditions of her life, the vistas of new relationships disclosed by every phrase, made her communications as impersonal as a piece of journalism. It was as though the state, the world, indeed, had taken her off his hands, assuming the maintenance of a temperament that had long exhausted his slender store of reciprocity.

In the retrospective light shed by the letters he was blinded to their specific meaning. He was not a man who concerned himself with literature, and they had been to him, at first, simply the extension of her brilliant talk, later the dreaded vehicle of a tragic importunity. He knew, of course, that they were wonderful; that, unlike the authors who give their essence to the public and keep only a dry rind for their friends, Mrs Aubyn had stored of her rarest vintage for this hidden sacrament of tenderness. Sometimes, indeed, he had been oppressed, humiliated almost, by the multiplicity of her allusions, the wide scope of her interests, her persistence in forcing her superabundance of thought and emotion into the shallow receptacle of his sympathy; but he had never thought of the letters objectively, as the production of a distinguished woman; had never measured the literary significance of her oppressive prodigality. He was almost frightened now at the wealth in his hands; the obligation of her love had never weighed on him like this gift of her imagination: it was as though he had accepted from her something to which even a reciprocal tenderness could not have justified his claim.

He sat a long time staring at the scattered pages on his desk; and in the sudden realisation of what they meant he could almost fancy some alchemistic process changing them to gold as he stared.

He had the sense of not being alone in the room, of the presence of another self observing from without the stirring of subconscious impulses that sent flushes of humiliation to his forehead. At length he stood up, and with the gesture of a man who wishes to give outward expression to his purpose – to establish, as it were, a moral alibi – swept the letters into a heap and carried them towards the grate. But it would have taken too long to burn all the packets. He turned back to the table and one by one fitted the pages into their envelopes; then he tied up the letters and put them back into the locked drawer.

3

It was one of the laws of Glennard's intercourse with Miss Trent that he always went to see her the day after he had resolved to give her up. There was a special charm about the moments thus snatched from the jaws of renunciation; and his sense of their significance was on this occasion so keen that he hardly noticed the added gravity of her welcome.

His feeling for her had become so vital a part of him that her nearness had the quality of imperceptibly readjusting his point of view, of making the jumbled phenomena of experience fall at once into a rational perspective. In this redistribution of values the sombre retrospect of the previous evening shrank to a mere cloud on the edge of consciousness. Perhaps the only service an unloved woman can render the man she loves is to enhance and prolong his illusions about her rival. It was the fate of Margaret Aubyn's memory to serve as a foil to Miss Trent's presence, and never had the poor lady thrown her successor into more vivid relief.

Miss Trent had the charm of still waters that are felt to be renewed by rapid currents. Her attention spread a tranquil surface to the demonstrations of others, and it was only in days of storm that one felt the pressure of the tides. This inscrutable composure was perhaps her chief grace in Glennard's eyes. Reserve, in some natures, implies merely the locking of empty rooms or the dissimulation of awkward encumbrances; but Miss Trent's reticence was to Glennard like the closed door to the sanctuary, and his certainty of divining the hidden treasure made him content to remain outside in the happy expectancy of the neophyte.

'You didn't come to the opera last night,' she began, in the tone that seemed always rather to record a fact than to offer a reflection on it.

He answered with a discouraged gesture. 'What was the use? We couldn't have talked.'

'Not as well as here,' she assented, adding, after a meditative pause, 'As you didn't come I talked to Aunt Virginia instead.'

'Ah!' he returned, the fact being hardly striking enough to detach him from the contemplation of her hands, which had fallen, as was their wont, into an attitude full of plastic possibilities. One felt them to be hands that, moving only to some purpose, were capable of intervals of serene inaction.

'We had a long talk,' Miss Trent went on; and she waited again before adding, with the increased absence of stress that marked her graver communications, 'Aunt Virginia wants me to go abroad with her.'

Glennard looked up with a start. 'Abroad? When?'

'Now – next month. To be gone two years.'

He permitted himself a movement of tender derision. 'Does she really? Well, I want you to go abroad with *me* – for any number of years. Which offer do you accept?'

'Only one of them seems to require immediate consideration,' she returned, with a smile.

Glennard looked at her again. 'You're not thinking of it?'

Her gaze dropped and she unclasped her hands. Her movements were so rare that they might have been said to italicise her words. 'Aunt Virginia talked to me very seriously. It will be a great relief to Mother and the others to have me provided for in that way for two years. I must think of that, you know.' She glanced down at her gown which, under a renovated surface, dated back to the first days of Glennard's wooing. 'I try not to cost much – but I do.'

'Good Lord!' Glennard groaned.

They sat silent till at length she gently took up the

argument. 'As the eldest, you know, I'm bound to consider these things. Women are such a burden. Jim does what he can for Mother, but with his own children to provide for it isn't very much. You see, we're all poor together.'

'Your aunt isn't. She might help your mother.'

'She does – in her own way.'

'Exactly – that's the rich relation all over! You may be miserable in any way you like, but if you're to be happy you must be so in her way – and in her old gowns.'

'I could be very happy in Aunt Virginia's old gowns,' Miss Trent interposed.

'Abroad, you mean?'

'I mean wherever I felt that I was helping. And my going abroad will help.'

'Of course – I see that. And I see your considerateness in putting its advantages negatively.'

'Negatively?'

'In dwelling simply on what the going will take you from, not on what it will bring you to. It means a lot to a woman, of course, to get away from a life like this.' He summed up in a disparaging glance the background of indigent furniture. 'The question is how you'll like coming back to it.'

She seemed to accept the full consequences of his thought. 'I only know I don't like leaving it.'

He flung back sombrely, 'You don't even put it conditionally then?'

Her gaze deepened. 'On what?'

He stood up and walked across the room. Then he came back and paused before her. 'On the alternative of marrying me.'

The slow colour – even her blushes seemed deliberate – rose to her lower lids; her lips stirred, but the words resolved themselves into a smile and she waited.

He took another turn, with the thwarted step of the man whose nervous exasperation escapes through his muscles.

'And to think that in fifteen years I shall have a big practice!'

Her eyes triumphed for him. 'In less!'

'The cursed irony of it! What do I care for the man I shall be then? It's slaving one's life away for a stranger!' He took her hands abruptly. 'You'll go to Cannes, I suppose, or Monte Carlo? I heard Hollingsworth say today that he meant to take his yacht over to the Mediterranean –'

She released herself. 'If you think that –'

'I don't. I almost wish I did. It would be easier, I mean.' He broke off incoherently. 'I believe your Aunt Virginia does, though. She somehow connotes Hollingsworth and the Mediterranean.' He caught her hands again. 'Alexa – if we could manage a little hole somewhere out of town?'

'Could we?' she sighed, half yielding.

'In one of those places where they make jokes about the mosquitoes,' he pressed her. 'Could you get on with one servant?'

'Could you get on without varnished boots?'

'Promise me you won't go, then!'

'What are you thinking of, Stephen?'

'I don't know,' he stammered, the question giving un-expected form to his intention. 'It's all in the air yet, of course; but I picked up a tip the other day –'

'You're not speculating?' she cried, with a kind of superstitious terror.

'Lord, no. This is a sure thing – I almost wish it wasn't; I mean if I can work it –' He had a sudden vision of the comprehensiveness of the temptation. If only he had been less sure of Dinslow! His assurance gave the situation the base element of safety.

'I don't understand you,' she faltered.

'Trust me, instead!' he adjured her, with sudden energy; and turning on her abruptly, 'If you go, you know, you go free,' he concluded.

She drew back, paling a little. 'Why do you make it harder for me?'

'To make it easier for myself,' he retorted.

4

The next afternoon Glennard, leaving his office earlier than usual, turned, on his way home, into one of the public libraries.

He had the place to himself at that closing hour, and the librarian was able to give an undivided attention to his tentative request for letters – collections of letters. The librarian suggested Walpole[1].

'I meant women – women's letters.'

The librarian proffered Hannah More and Miss Martineau.[2]

Glennard cursed his own inarticulateness. 'I mean letters to – to some one person – a man; their husband – or –'

'Ah,' said the inspired librarian, 'Eloise and Abailard.[3]'

'Well – something a little nearer, perhaps,' said Glennard, with lightness. 'Didn't Mérimée[4] –'

'The lady's letters, in that case, were not published.'

'Of course not,' said Glennard, vexed at his blunder.

'There are George Sand's letters to Flaubert.[5]'

'Ah!' Glennard hesitated. 'Was she – were they –?' He chafed at his own ignorance of the sentimental bypaths of literature.

'If you want love letters, perhaps some of the French eighteenth-century correspondences might suit you better – Mademoiselle Aïssé or Madame de Sabran –⁶'

But Glennard insisted. 'I want something modern – English or American. I want to look something up,' he lamely concluded.

The librarian could only suggest George Eliot.

'Well, give me some of the French things, then – and I'll have Mérimée's letters. It was the woman who published them, wasn't it?'

He caught up his armful, transferring it, on the doorstep, to a cab which carried him to his rooms. He dined alone, hurriedly, at a small restaurant near by, and returned at once to his books.

Late that night, as he undressed, he wondered what contemptible impulse had forced from him his last words to Alexa Trent. It was bad enough to interfere with the girl's chances by hanging about her to the obvious exclusion of other men, but it was worse to seem to justify his weakness by dressing up the future in delusive ambiguities. He saw himself sinking from depth to depth of sentimental cowardice in his reluctance to renounce his hold on her; and it filled him with self-disgust to think that the highest feeling of which he supposed himself capable was blent with such base elements.

His awakening was hardly cheered by the sight of her writing. He tore her note open and took in the few lines – she seldom exceeded the first page – with the lucidity of apprehension that is the forerunner of evil.

My aunt sails on Saturday and I must give her my answer the day after tomorrow. Please don't come till then – I want

to think the question over by myself. I know I ought to go.
Won't you help me to be reasonable?

It was settled, then. Well, he would be reasonable; he wouldn't stand in her way; he would let her go. For two years he had been living some other, luckier man's life; the time had come when he must drop back into his own. He no longer tried to look ahead, to grope his way through the endless labyrinth of his material difficulties; a sense of dull resignation closed in on him like a fog.

'Hello, Glennard!' a voice said, as an electric car, late that afternoon, dropped him at an uptown corner.

He looked up and met the interrogative smile of Barton Flamel, who stood on the kerbstone watching the retreating car with the eye of a man philosophic enough to remember that it will be followed by another.

Glennard felt his usual impulse of pleasure at meeting Flamel; but it was not in this case curtailed by the reaction of contempt that habitually succeeded it. Probably even the few men who had known Flamel since his youth could have given no good reason for the vague mistrust that he inspired. Some people are judged by their actions, others by their ideas; and perhaps the shortest way of defining Flamel is to say that his well-known leniency of view was vaguely divined to include himself. Simple minds may have resented the discovery that his opinions were based on his perceptions; but there was certainly no more definite charge against him than that implied in the doubt as to how he would behave in an emergency, and his company was looked upon as one of those mildly unwholesome dissipations to which the prudent may occasionally yield. It now offered itself to Glennard as an easy escape from the obsession of moral problems, which somehow could no more be worn in Flamel's presence than a surplice in the street.

'Where are you going? To the club?' Flamel asked; adding, as the younger man assented, 'Why not come to my studio instead? You'll see one bore instead of twenty.'

The apartment which Flamel described as his studio showed, as its one claim to the designation, a perennially empty easel, the rest of its space being filled with the evidences of a comprehensive dilettantism. Against this background, which seemed the visible expression of its owner's intellectual tolerance, rows of fine books detached themselves with a prominence, showing them to be Flamel's chief care.

Glennard glanced with the eye of untrained curiosity at the lines of warm-toned morocco, while his host busied himself with the uncorking of Apollinaris.

'You've got a splendid lot of books,' he said.

'They're fairly decent,' the other assented, in the curt tone of the collector who will not talk of his passion for fear of talking of nothing else; then, as Glennard, his hands in his pockets, began to stroll perfunctorily down the long line of bookcases: 'Some men,' Flamel irresistibly added, 'think of books merely as tools, others as tooling. I'm between the two; there are days when I use them as scenery, other days when I want them as society; so that, as you see, my library represents a makeshift compromise between looks and brains, and the collectors look down on me almost as much as the students.'

Glennard, without answering, was mechanically taking one book after another from the shelves. His hands slipped curiously over the smooth covers and the noiseless subsidence of opening pages. Suddenly he came on a thin volume of faded manuscript.

'What's this?' he asked, with a listless sense of wonder.

'Ah, you're at my manuscript shelf. I've been going in for that sort of thing lately.' Flamel came up and looked over his shoulders. 'That's a bit of Stendhal – one of the Italian stories – and here are some letters of Balzac to Madame Surville.'

Glennard took the book with sudden eagerness. 'Who was Madame Surville?'

'His sister.' He was conscious that Flamel was looking at him with the smile that was like an interrogation point. 'I didn't know you cared for this kind of thing.'

'I don't – at least I've never had the chance. Have you many collections of letters?'

'Lord, no – very few. I'm just beginning, and most of the interesting ones are out of my reach. Here's a queer little collection, though – the rarest thing I've got – half a dozen of Shelley's letters to Harriet Westbrook.[7] I had a devil of a time getting them – a lot of collectors were after them.'

Glennard, taking the volume from his hand, glanced with a kind of repugnance at the interleaving of yellow criss-crossed sheets. 'She was the one who drowned herself, wasn't she?'

Flamel nodded. 'I suppose that little episode adds about fifty per cent to their value,' he said, meditatively.

Glennard laid the book down. He wondered why he had joined Flamel. He was in no humour to be amused by the older man's talk, and a recrudescence of personal misery rose about him like an icy tide.

'I believe I must take myself off,' he said. 'I'd forgotten an engagement.'

He turned to go; but almost at the same moment he was conscious of a duality of intention wherein his apparent wish to leave revealed itself as a last effort of the will against the overmastering desire to stay and unbosom himself to Flamel.

The older man, as though divining the conflict, laid a detaining pressure on his arm.

'Won't the engagement keep? Sit down and try one of these cigars. I don't often have the luck of seeing you here.'

'I'm rather driven just now,' said Glennard, vaguely. He found himself seated again, and Flamel had pushed to his side a low stand holding a bottle of Apollinaris and a decanter of cognac.

Flamel, thrown back in his capacious armchair, surveyed him through a cloud of smoke with the comfortable tolerance of the man to whom no inconsistencies need be explained. Connivance was implicit in the air. It was the kind of atmosphere in which the outrageous loses its edge. Glennard felt a gradual relaxing of his nerves.

'I suppose one has to pay a lot for letters like that?' he heard himself asking, with a glance in the direction of the volume he had laid aside.

'Oh, so-so – depends on circumstances.' Flamel viewed him thoughtfully. 'Are you thinking of collecting?'

Glennard laughed. 'Lord, no. The other way round.'

'Selling?'

'Oh, I hardly know. I was thinking of a poor chap –'

Flamel filled the pause with a nod of interest.

'A poor chap I used to know – who died – he died last year – and who left me a lot of letters, letters he thought a great deal of – he was fond of me and left 'em to me outright, with the idea, I suppose, that they might benefit me somehow – I don't know – I'm not much up on such things –' He reached his hand to the tall glass his host had filled.

'A collection of autograph letters, eh? Any big names?'

'Oh, only one name. They're all letters written to him – by one person, you understand; a woman, in fact –'

'Oh, a woman,' said Flamel, negligently.

Glennard was nettled by his obvious loss of interest. 'I rather think they'd attract a good deal of notice if they were published.'

Flamel still looked uninterested. 'Love letters, I suppose?'

'Oh, just – the letters a woman would write to a man she knew well. They were tremendous friends, he and she.'

'And she wrote a clever letter?'

'Clever? It was Margaret Aubyn.'

A great silence filled the room. It seemed to Glennard that the words had burst from him as blood gushes from a wound.

'Great Scott!' said Flamel, sitting up. 'A collection of Margaret Aubyn's letters? Did you say *you* had them?'

'They were left me – by my friend.'

'I see. Was he – well, no matter. You're to be congratulated, at any rate. What are you going to do with them?'

Glennard stood up with a sense of weariness in all his bones. 'Oh, I don't know. I haven't thought much about it. I just happened to see that some fellow was writing her life –'

'Joslin; yes. You didn't think of giving them to him?'

Glennard had lounged across the room and stood staring up at a bronze Bacchus who drooped his garlanded head above the pediment of an Italian cabinet. 'What ought I to do? You're just the fellow to advise me.' He felt the blood in his cheek as he spoke.

Flamel sat with meditative eye. 'What do you *want* to do with them?' he asked.

'I want to publish them,' said Glennard, swinging round with sudden energy. 'If I can –'

'If you can? They're yours, you say?'

'They're mine fast enough. There's no one to prevent – I mean there are no restrictions –' He was arrested by the sense that these accumulated proofs of impunity might precisely stand as the strongest check on his action.

'And Mrs Aubyn had no family, I believe?'

'No.'

'Then I don't see who's to interfere,' said Flamel, studying his cigar-tip.

Glennard had turned his unseeing stare on an ecstatic St Catherine framed in tarnished gilding.

'It's just this way,' he began again, with an effort. 'When letters are as personal as – as these of my friend's… Well, I don't mind telling you that the cash would make a heap of difference to me; such a lot that it rather obscures my judgement – the fact is, if I could lay my hand on a few thousand now, I could get into a big thing, and without appreciable risk; and I'd like to know whether you think I'd be justified – under the circumstances…' He paused, with a dry throat. It seemed to him at the moment that it would be impossible for him ever to sink lower in his own estimation. He was in truth less ashamed of weighing the temptation than of submitting his scruples to a man like Flamel, and affecting to appeal to sentiments of delicacy on the absence of which he had consciously reckoned. But he had reached a point where each word seemed to compel another, as each wave in a stream is forced forward by the pressure behind it; and before Flamel could speak he had faltered out – 'You don't think people could say… could criticise the man…'

'But the man's dead, isn't he?'

'He's dead – yes; but can I assume the responsibility without –'

Flamel hesitated; and almost immediately Glennard's scruples gave way to irritation. If at this hour Flamel were to affect an inopportune reluctance –!

The older man's answer reassured him. 'Why need you assume any responsibility? Your name won't appear, of course; and as to your friend's, I don't see why his should either. He wasn't a celebrity himself, I suppose?'

'No, no.'

'Then the letters can be addressed to Mr Blank. Doesn't that make it all right?'

Glennard's hesitation revived. 'For the public, yes. But I don't see that it alters the case for me. The question is, ought I to publish them at all?'

'Of course you ought to.' Flamel spoke with invigorating emphasis. 'I doubt if you'd be justified in keeping them back. Anything of Margaret Aubyn's is more or less public property by this time. She's too great for any one of us. I was only wondering how you could use them to the best advantage – to yourself, I mean. How many are there?'

'Oh, a lot; perhaps a hundred – I haven't counted. There may be more…'

'Gad! What a haul! When were they written?'

'I don't know – that is – they corresponded for years. What's the odds?' He moved towards his hat with a vague impulse of flight.

'It all counts,' said Flamel, imperturbably. 'A long corres-pondence – one, I mean, that covers a great deal of time – is obviously worth more than if the same number of letters had been written within a year. At any rate, you won't give them to Joslin? They'd fill a book, wouldn't they?'

'I suppose so. I don't know how much it takes to fill a book.'

'Not love letters, you say?'

'Why?' flashed from Glennard.

'Oh, nothing – only the big public is sentimental, and if

30

they *were* – why, you could get any money for Margaret Aubyn's love letters.'

Glennard was silent.

'Are the letters interesting in themselves? I mean apart from the association with her name?'

'I'm no judge.' Glennard took up his hat and thrust himself into his overcoat. 'I dare say I shan't do anything about it. And, Flamel – you won't mention this to anyone?'

'Lord, no. Well, I congratulate you. You've got a big thing.' Flamel was smiling at him from the hearth.

Glennard, on the threshold, forced a response to the smile, while he questioned with loitering indifference – 'Financially, eh?'

'Rather; I should say so.'

Glennard's hand lingered on the knob. 'How much – should you say? You know about such things.'

'Oh, I should have to see the letters; but I should say – well, if you've got enough to fill a book and they're fairly readable, and the book is brought out at the right time – say ten thousand down from the publisher, and possibly one or two more in royalties. If you got the publishers bidding against each other you might do even better; but of course I'm talking in the dark.'

'Of course,' said Glennard, with sudden dizziness. His hand had slipped from the knob and he stood staring down at the exotic spirals of the Persian rug beneath his feet.

'I'd have to see the letters,' Flamel repeated.

'Of course – you'd have to see them…' Glennard stammered; and, without turning, he flung over his shoulder an inarticulate goodbye…

5

The little house, as Glennard strolled up to it between the trees, seemed no more than a gay tent pitched against the sunshine. It had the crispness of a freshly starched summer gown, and the geraniums on the veranda bloomed as simultaneously as the flowers in a bonnet. The garden was prospering absurdly. Seed they had sown at random – amid laughing counter-charges of incompetence – had shot up in fragrant defiance of their blunders. He smiled to see the clematis unfolding its punctual wings about the porch. The tiny lawn was smooth as a shaven cheek, and a crimson rambler mounted to the nursery window of a baby who never cried. A breeze shook the awning above the tea table, and his wife, as he drew near, could be seen bending above a kettle that was just about to boil. So vividly did the whole scene suggest the painted bliss of a stage setting that it would have been hardly surprising to see her step forward among the flowers and trill out her virtuous happiness from the veranda rail.

The stale heat of the long day in town, the dusty prom-iscuity of the suburban train, were now but the requisite foil to an evening of scented breezes and tranquil talk. They had been married more than a year, and each homecoming still reflected the freshness of their first day together. If, indeed, their happiness had a flaw, it was in resembling too closely the bright impermanence of their surroundings. Their love as yet was but the gay tent of holidaymakers.

His wife looked up with a smile. The country life suited her, and her beauty had gained depth from a stillness in which certain faces might have grown opaque.

'Are you very tired?' she asked, pouring his tea.

'Just enough to enjoy this.' He rose from the chair in which he had thrown himself and bent over the tray for his cream. 'You've had a visitor?' he commented, noticing a half-empty cup beside her own.

'Only Mr Flamel,' she said, indifferently.

'Flamel? Again?'

She answered without show of surprise. 'He left just now. His yacht is down at Laurel Bay, and he borrowed a trap of the Dreshams to drive over here.'

Glennard made no comment, and she went on, leaning her head back against the cushions of her bamboo seat, 'He wants us to go for a sail with him next Sunday.'

Glennard meditatively stirred his tea. He was trying to think of the most natural and unartificial thing to say, and his voice seemed to come from the outside, as though he were speaking behind a marionette. 'Do you want to?'

'Just as you please,' she said, compliantly. No affectation of indifference could have been as baffling as her compliance. Glennard, of late, was beginning to feel that the surface which, a year ago, he had taken for a sheet of clear glass, might, after all, be a mirror reflecting merely his own conception of what lay behind it.

'Do you like Flamel?' he suddenly asked; to which, still engaged with her tea, she returned the feminine answer: 'I thought you did.'

'I do, of course,' he agreed, vexed at his own incorrigible tendency to magnify Flamel's importance by hovering about the topic. 'A sail would be rather jolly; let's go.'

She made no reply and he drew forth the rolled-up evening papers which he had thrust into his pocket on leaving the train. As he smoothed them out, his own countenance seemed to undergo the same process. He ran his eye down the list of stocks, and Flamel's importunate personality receded behind the rows of figures pushing forward into notice like so many bearers of good news. Glennard's investments were flowering like his garden: the driest shares blossomed into dividends, and a golden harvest awaited his sickle.

He glanced at his wife with the tranquil air of a man who digests good luck as naturally as the dry ground absorbs a shower. 'Things are looking uncommonly well. I believe we shall be able to go to town for two or three months next winter if we can find something cheap.'

She smiled luxuriously: it was pleasant to be able to say, with an air of balancing relative advantages, 'Really, on the baby's account I shall be almost sorry; but if we do go, there's Kate Erskine's house... she'll let us have it for almost nothing...'

'Well, write her about it,' he recommended, his eyes travelling on in search of the weather report. He had turned to the wrong page; and suddenly a line of black characters leapt out at him as from an ambush.

Margaret Aubyn's Letters
Two volumes. Out today. First edition of five thousand sold out before leaving the press. Second edition ready next week. The book of the year...

He looked up stupidly. His wife still sat with her head thrown back, her pure profile detached against the cushions. She was smiling a little over the prospect his last words had opened. Behind her head shivers of sun and shade ran across the striped awning. A row of maples and a privet hedge hid their neighbour's gables, giving them undivided possession of their leafy half-acre; and life, a moment before, had been like

34

their plot of ground, shut off, hedged in from importunities, impenetrably his and hers. Now it seemed to him that every maple leaf, every privet bud, was a relentless human gaze, pressing close upon their privacy. It was as though they sat in a brightly lit room, uncurtained from a darkness full of hostile watchers… His wife still smiled; and her unconsciousness of danger seemed, in some horrible way, to put her beyond the reach of rescue…

He had not known that it would be like this. After the first odious weeks, spent in preparing the letters for publication, in submitting them to Flamel, and in negotiating with the publishers, the transaction had dropped out of his consciousness into that unvisited limbo to which we relegate the deeds we would rather not have done but have no notion of undoing. From the moment he had obtained Miss Trent's promise not to sail with her aunt, he had tried to imagine himself irrevocably committed. After that, he argued, his first duty was to her – she had become his conscience. The sum obtained from the publishers by Flamel's adroit manipulations, and opportunely transferred to Dinslow's successful venture, already yielded a return which, combined with Glennard's professional earnings, took the edge of compulsion from their way of living, making it appear the expression of a graceful preference for simplicity. It was the mitigated poverty which can subscribe to a review or two and have a few flowers on the dinner table. And already in a small way Glennard was beginning to feel the magnetic quality of prosperity. Clients who had passed his door in the hungry days sought it out now that it bore the name of a successful man. It was understood that a small inheritance, cleverly invested, was the source of his fortune; and there was a feeling that a man who could do so well for himself was likely to know how to turn over other people's money.

But it was in the more intimate reward of his wife's happiness that Glennard tasted the full flavour of success. Coming out of conditions so narrow that those he offered her seemed spacious, she fitted into her new life without any of those manifest efforts at adjustment that are as sore to a husband's pride as the critical rearrangement of the bridal furniture. She had given him, instead, the delicate pleasure of watching her expand like a sea-creature restored to its element, stretching out the atrophied tentacles of girlish vanity and enjoyment to the rising tide of opportunity. And somehow – in the windowless inner cell of his consciousness where self-criticism cowered – Glennard's course seemed justified by its merely material success. How could such a crop of innocent blessedness have sprung from tainted soil?

Now he had the injured sense of a man entrapped into a disadvantageous bargain. He had not known it would be like this; and a dull anger gathered at his heart. Anger against whom? Against his wife, for not knowing what he suffered? Against Flamel, for being the unconscious instrument of his wrongdoing? Or against that mute memory to which his own act had suddenly given a voice of accusation? Yes, that was it; and his punishment henceforth would be the presence, the inescapable presence, of the woman he had so persistently evaded. She would always be there now. It was as though he had married her instead of the other. It was what she had always wanted – to be with him – and she had gained her point at last…

He sprang up, as though in an impulse of flight… The sudden movement lifted his wife's lids, and she asked, in the incurious voice of the woman whose life is enclosed in a magic circle of prosperity – 'Any news?'

'No – none –' he said, roused to a sense of immediate peril. The papers lay scattered at his feet – what if she were to see them? He stretched his arm to gather them up, but his next thought showed him the futility of such concealment. The same advertisement would appear every day, for weeks to come, in every newspaper; how could he prevent her seeing it? He could not always be hiding the papers from her... Well, and what if she did see it? It would signify nothing to her, the chances were that she would never even read the book... As she ceased to be an element of fear in his calculations, the distance between them seemed to lessen and he took her again, as it were, into the circle of his conjugal protection... Yet a moment before he had almost hated her!... He laughed aloud at his senseless terrors... He was off his balance, decidedly...

'What are you laughing at?' she asked.

He explained, elaborately, that he was laughing at the recollection of an old woman in the train, an old woman with a lot of bundles, who couldn't find her ticket... But somehow, in the telling, the humour of the story seemed to evaporate, and he felt the conventionality of her smile. He glanced at his watch, 'Isn't it time to dress?'

She rose with serene reluctance. 'It's a pity to go in. The garden looks so lovely.'

They lingered side by side, surveying their domain. There was not space in it, at this hour, for the shadow of the elm tree in the angle of the hedge: it crossed the lawn, cut the flower-border in two, and ran up the side of the house to the nursery window. She bent to flick a caterpillar from the honeysuckle; then, as they turned indoors, 'If we mean to go on the yacht next Sunday,' she suggested, 'oughtn't you to let Mr Flamel know?'

Glennard's exasperation deflected suddenly. 'Of course I shall let him know. You always seem to imply that I'm going to do something rude to Flamel.'

The words reverberated through her silence; she had a way of thus leaving one space in which to contemplate one's folly at arm's length. Glennard turned on his heel and went upstairs. As he dropped into a chair before his dressing table he said to himself that in the last hour he had sounded the depths of his humiliation and that the lowest dregs of it, the very bottom-slime, was the hateful necessity of having always, as long as the two men lived, to be civil to Barton Flamel.

6

The week in town had been sultry, and the men, in the Sunday emancipation of white flannel and duck, filled the deckchairs of the yacht with their outstretched apathy, following, through a mist of cigarette smoke, the flitting inconsequences of the women. The party was a small one – Flamel had few intimate friends – but composed of more heterogeneous atoms than the little pools into which society usually runs. The reaction from the chief episode of his earlier life had bred in Glennard an uneasy distaste for any kind of personal saliency. Cleverness was useful in business; but in society it seemed to him as futile as the sham cascades formed by a stream that might have been used to drive a mill. He liked the collective point of view that goes with the civilised uniformity of dress clothes, and his wife's attitude implied the same preference; yet they found themselves slipping more and more into Flamel's intimacy. Alexa had once or twice said that she enjoyed meeting clever people; but her enjoyment took the negative form of a smiling receptivity; and

Glennard felt a growing preference for the kind of people who have their thinking done for them by the community.

Still, the deck of the yacht was a pleasant refuge from the heat on shore, and his wife's profile, serenely projected against the changing blue, lay on his retina like a cool hand on the nerves. He had never been more impressed by the kind of absoluteness that lifted her beauty above the transient effects of other women, making the most harmonious face seem an accidental collocation of features.

The ladies who directly suggested this comparison were of a kind accustomed to take similar risks with more gratifying results. Mrs Armiger had in fact long been the triumphant alternative of those who couldn't 'see' Alexa Glennard's looks; and Mrs Touchett's claims to consideration were founded on that distribution of effects which is the wonder of those who admire a highly cultivated country. The third lady of the trio which Glennard's fancy had put to such unflattering uses was bound by circumstances to support the claims of the other two. This was Mrs Dresham, the wife of the editor of the *Radiator*. Mrs Dresham was a lady who had rescued herself from social obscurity by assuming the role of her husband's exponent and interpreter; and Dresham's leisure being devoted to the cultivation of remarkable women, his wife's attitude committed her to the public celebration of their remarkableness. For the conceivable tedium of this duty, Mrs Dresham was repaid by the fact that there were people who took *her* for a remarkable woman; and who in turn probably purchased similar distinction with the small change of her reflected importance. As to the other ladies of the party, they were simply the wives of some of the men – the kind of women who expect to be talked to collectively and to have their questions left unanswered.

Mrs Armiger, the latest embodiment of Dresham's instinct for the remarkable, was an innocent beauty who for years had distilled dullness among a set of people now self-condemned by their inability to appreciate her. Under Dresham's tutelage she had developed into a 'thoughtful woman' who read his leaders in the *Radiator* and bought the works he recommended. When a new novel appeared, people wanted to know what Mrs Armiger thought of it; and a young gentleman who had made a trip in Touraine had recently inscribed to her the wide-margined result of his explorations.

Glennard, leaning back with his head against the rail and a slit of fugitive blue between his half-closed lids, vaguely wished she wouldn't spoil the afternoon by making people talk; though he reduced his annoyance to the minimum by not listening to what was said, there remained a latent irritation against the general futility of words.

His wife's gift of silence seemed to him the most vivid commentary on the clumsiness of speech as a means of intercourse, and his eyes had turned to her in renewed appreciation of this finer faculty when Mrs Armiger's voice abruptly brought home to him the underrated potentialities of language.

'You've read them, of course, Mrs Glennard?' he heard her ask; and, in reply to Alexa's vague interrogation – 'Why, the *Aubyn Letters* – it's the only book people are talking of this week.'

Mrs Dresham immediately saw her advantage. 'You *haven't* read them? How very extraordinary! As Mrs Armiger says, the book's in the air: one breathes it in like the influenza.'

Glennard sat motionless, watching his wife.

'Perhaps it hasn't reached the suburbs yet,' she said, with her unruffled smile.

'Oh, *do* let me come to you, then!' Mrs Touchett cried; 'anything for a change of air! I'm positively sick of the book and I can't put it down. Can't you sail us beyond its reach, Mr Flamel?'

Flamel shook his head. 'Not even with this breeze. Literature travels faster than steam nowadays. And the worst of it is that we can't any of us give up reading; it's as insidious as a vice and as tiresome as a virtue.'

'I believe it *is* a vice, almost, to read such a book as the *Letters*,' said Mrs Touchett. 'It's the woman's soul, absolutely torn up by the roots – her whole self laid bare; and to a man who evidently didn't care; who couldn't have cared. I don't mean to read another line: it's too much like listening at a keyhole.'

'But if she wanted it published?'

'Wanted it? How do we know she did?'

'Why, I heard she'd left the letters to the man – whoever he is – with directions that they should be published after his death –'

'I don't believe it,' Mrs Touchett declared.

'He's dead then, is he?' one of the men asked.

'Why, you don't suppose if he were alive he could ever hold up his head again, with these letters being read by everybody?' Mrs Touchett protested. 'It must have been horrible enough to know they'd been written to him; but to publish them! No man could have done it and no woman could have told him to –'

'Oh, come, come,' Dresham judicially interposed; 'after all, they're not love letters.'

'No – that's the worst of it; they're unloved letters,' Mrs Touchett retorted.

'Then, obviously, she needn't have written them; whereas

the man, poor devil, could hardly help receiving them.'

'Perhaps he counted on the public to save him the trouble of reading them,' said young Hartly, who was in the cynical stage.

Mrs Armiger turned her reproachful loveliness to Dresham. 'From the way you defend him, I believe you know who he is.'

Everyone looked at Dresham, and his wife smiled with the superior air of the woman who is in her husband's professional secrets. Dresham shrugged his shoulders.

'What have I said to defend him?'

'You called him a poor devil – you pitied him.'

'A man who could let Margaret Aubyn write to him in that way? Of course I pity him.'

'Then you *must* know who he is,' cried Mrs Armiger, with a triumphant air of penetration.

Hartly and Flamel laughed and Dresham shook his head. 'No one knows; not even the publishers; so they tell me at least.'

'So they tell you to tell us,' Hartly astutely amended; and Mrs Armiger added, with the appearance of carrying the argument a point further, 'But even if *he's* dead and *she's* dead, somebody must have given the letters to the publishers.'

'A little bird, probably,' said Dresham, smiling indulgently on her deduction.

'A little bird of prey then – a vulture, I should say –' another man interpolated.

'Oh, I'm not with you there,' said Dresham, easily. 'Those letters belonged to the public.'

'How can any letters belong to the public that weren't written to the public?' Mrs Touchett interposed.

'Well, these were, in a sense. A personality as big as Margaret Aubyn's belongs to the world. Such a mind is part of the general fund of thought. It's the penalty of greatness – one becomes a *monument historique*. Posterity pays the cost of keeping one up, but on condition that one is always open to the public.'

'I don't see that that exonerates the man who gives up the keys of the sanctuary, as it were.'

'Who *was* he?' another voice enquired.

'Who was he? Oh, nobody, I fancy – the letter-box, the slit in the wall through which the letters passed to posterity…'

'But she never meant them for posterity!'

'A woman shouldn't write such letters if she doesn't mean them to be published…'

'She shouldn't write them to such a man!' Mrs Touchett scornfully corrected.

'I never keep letters,' said Mrs Armiger, under the obvious impression that she was contributing a valuable point to the discussion.

There was a general laugh, and Flamel, who had not spoken, said, lazily, 'You women are too incurably subjective. I venture to say that most men would see in those letters merely their immense literary value, their significance as documents. The personal side doesn't count where there's so much else.'

'Oh, we all know you haven't any principles,' Mrs Armiger declared; and Alexa Glennard, lifting an indolent smile, said, 'I shall never write you a love letter, Mr Flamel.'

Glennard moved away impatiently. Such talk was as tedious as the buzzing of gnats. He wondered why his wife had wanted to drag him on such a senseless expedition… He hated Flamel's crowd – and what business had Flamel himself to interfere in that way, standing up for the publication of the letters as though Glennard needed his defence?…

Glennard turned his head and saw that Flamel had drawn a seat to Alexa's elbow and was speaking to her in a low tone.

The other groups had scattered, straying in twos along the deck. It came over Glennard that he should never again be able to see Flamel speaking to his wife without the sense of sick mistrust that now loosened his joints...

Alexa, the next morning, over their early breakfast, surprised her husband by an unexpected request.

'Will you bring me those letters from town?' she asked.

'What letters?' he said, putting down his cup. He felt himself as vulnerable as a man who is lunged at in the dark.

'Mrs Aubyn's. The book they were all talking about yesterday.'

Glennard, carefully measuring his second cup of tea, said, with deliberation, 'I didn't know you cared about that sort of thing.'

She was, in fact, not a great reader, and a new book seldom reached her till it was, so to speak, on the home stretch; but she replied, with a gentle tenacity, 'I think it would interest me because I read her life last year.'

'Her life? Where did you get that?'

'Someone lent it to me when it came out – Mr Flamel, I think.'

His first impulse was to exclaim, 'Why the devil do you borrow books of Flamel? I can buy you all you want –' but he felt himself irresistibly forced into an attitude of smiling compliance. 'Flamel always has the newest books going, hasn't he? You must be careful, by the way, about returning what he lends you. He's rather crotchety about his library.'

'Oh, I'm always very careful,' she said, with a touch of competence that struck him; and she added, as he caught up his hat: 'Don't forget the letters.'

Why had she asked for the book? Was her sudden wish to

44

see it the result of some hint of Flamel's? The thought turned Glennard sick, but he preserved sufficient lucidity to tell himself, a moment later, that his last hope of self-control would be lost if he yielded to the temptation of seeing a hidden purpose in everything she said and did. How much Flamel guessed, he had no means of divining; nor could he predicate, from what he knew of the man, to what use his inferences might be put. The very qualities that had made Flamel a useful adviser made him the most dangerous of accomplices. Glennard felt himself agrope among alien forces that his own act had set in motion…

Alexa was a woman of few requirements; but her wishes, even in trifles, had a definiteness that distinguished them from the fluid impulses of her kind. He knew that, having once asked for the book, she would not forget it; and he put aside, as an ineffectual expedient, his momentary idea of applying for it at the circulating library and telling her that all the copies were out. If the book was to be bought it had better be bought at once. He left his office earlier than usual and turned in at the first bookshop on his way to the train. The show-window was stacked with conspicuously lettered volumes. *Margaret Aubyn* flashed back at him in endless repetition. He plunged into the shop and came on a counter where the name reiterated itself on row after row of bindings. It seemed to have driven the rest of literature to the back shelves. He caught up a copy, tossing the money to an astonished clerk, who pursued him to the door with the unheeded offer to wrap up the volumes.

In the street he was seized with a sudden apprehension. What if he were to meet Flamel? The thought was intolerable. He called a cab and drove straight to the station where, amid the palm-leaf fans of a perspiring crowd, he waited a long half-hour for his train to start.

He had thrust a volume in either pocket and in the train he dared not draw them out; but the detested words leapt at him from the folds of the evening paper. The air seemed full of Margaret Aubyn's name. The motion of the train set it dancing up and down on the page of a magazine that a man in front of him was reading…

At the door he was told that Mrs Glennard was still out, and he went upstairs to his room and dragged the books from his pocket. They lay on the table before him like live things that he feared to touch… At length he opened the first volume. A familiar letter sprang out at him, each word quickened by its glaring garb of type. The little broken phrases fled across the page like wounded animals in the open… It was a horrible sight… A battue of helpless things driven savagely out of shelter. He had not known it would be like this…

He understood now that, at the moment of selling the letters, he had viewed the transaction solely as it affected himself: as an unfortunate blemish on an otherwise presentable record. He had scarcely considered the act in relation to Margaret Aubyn; for death, if it hallows, also makes innocuous. Glennard's god was a god of the living, of the immediate, the actual, the tangible; all his days he had lived in the presence of that god, heedless of the divinities who, below the surface of our deeds and passions, silently forge the fatal weapons of the dead.

7

A knock roused him and, looking up, he saw his wife. He met her glance in silence, and she faltered out, 'Are you ill?'

The words restored his self-possession. 'Ill? Of course not.

46

They told me you were out and I came upstairs.'

The books lay between them on the table; he wondered when she would see them. She lingered tentatively on the threshold, with the air of leaving his explanation on his hands. She was not the kind of woman who could be counted on to fortify an excuse by appearing to dispute it.

'Where have you been?' Glennard asked, moving forward so that he obstructed her vision of the books.

'I walked over to the Dreshams' for tea.'

'I can't think what you see in those people,' he said, with a shrug; adding, uncontrollably – 'I suppose Flamel was there?'

'No; he left on the yacht this morning.'

An answer so obstructing to the natural escape of his irritation left Glennard with no momentary resource but that of strolling impatiently to the window. As her eyes followed him they lit on the books.

'Ah, you've brought them! I'm so glad,' she said.

He answered over his shoulder, 'For a woman who never reads you make the most astounding exceptions!'

Her smile was an exasperating concession to the probability that it had been hot in town or that something had bothered him.

'Do you mean it's not nice to want to read the book?' she asked. 'It was not nice to publish it, certainly; but after all, I'm not responsible for that, am I?' She paused, and, as he made no answer, went on, still smiling, 'I do read sometimes, you know; and I'm very fond of Margaret Aubyn's books. I was reading *Pomegranate Seed* when we first met. Don't you remember? It was then you told me all about her.'

Glennard had turned back into the room and stood staring at his wife. 'All about her?' he repeated, and with the words remembrance came to him. He had found Miss Trent one afternoon with the novel in her hand, and moved by the lover's fatuous impulse to associate himself in some way with whatever fills the mind of the beloved, had broken through his habitual silence about the past. Rewarded by the consciousness of figuring impressively in Miss Trent's imagination, he had gone on from one anecdote to another, reviving dormant details of his old Hillbridge life, and pasturing his vanity on the eagerness with which she received his reminiscences of a being already clothed in the impersonality of greatness.

The incident had left no trace in his mind; but it sprang up now like an old enemy, the more dangerous for having been forgotten. The instinct of self-preservation – sometimes the most perilous that man can exercise – made him awkwardly declare: 'Oh, I used to see her at people's houses, that was all;' and her silence as usual leaving room for a multiplication of blunders, he added, with increased indifference, 'I simply can't see what you can find to interest you in such a book.'

She seemed to consider this intently. 'You've read it, then?'

'I glanced at it – I never read such things.'

'Is it true that she didn't wish the letters to be published?'

Glennard felt the sudden dizziness of the mountaineer on a narrow ledge, and with it the sense that he was lost if he looked more than a step ahead.

'I'm sure I don't know,' he said; then, summoning a smile, he passed his hand through her arm. '*I* didn't have tea at the Dreshams', you know; won't you give me some now?' he suggested.

That evening Glennard, under pretext of work to be done, shut himself into the small study opening off the drawing room. As he gathered up his papers he said to his wife: 'You're not going to sit indoors on such a night as this? I'll join you presently outside.'

But she had drawn her armchair to the lamp. 'I want to look at my book,' she said, taking up the first volume of the *Letters*.

Glennard, with a shrug, withdrew into the study. 'I'm going to shut the door; I want to be quiet,' he explained from the threshold; and she nodded without lifting her eyes from the book.

He sank into a chair, staring aimlessly at the outspread papers. How was he to work, while on the other side of the door she sat with that volume in her hand? The door did not shut her out – he saw her distinctly, felt her close to him in a contact as painful as the pressure on a bruise.

The sensation was part of the general strangeness that made him feel like a man waking from a long sleep to find himself in an unknown country among people of alien tongue. We live in our own souls as in an unmapped region, a few acres of which we have cleared for our habitation; while of the nature of those nearest us we know but the boundaries that march with ours. Of the points in his wife's character not in direct contact with his own, Glennard now discerned his ignorance; and the baffling sense of her remoteness was intensified by the discovery that, in one way, she was closer to him than ever before. As one may live for years in happy unconsciousness of the possession of a sensitive nerve, he had lived beside his wife unaware that her individuality had become a part of the texture of his life, ineradicable as some growth on a vital organ; and he now felt himself at once incapable of forecasting her judgement and powerless to evade its effects.

To escape, the next morning, the confidences of the breakfast table, he went to town earlier than usual. His wife, who read slowly, was given to talking over what she read, and at present his first object in life was to postpone the inevitable discussion of the letters. This instinct of protection, in the afternoon, on his way up town, guided him to the club in search of a man who might be persuaded to come out to the country to dine. The only man in the club was Flamel.

Glennard, as he heard himself almost involuntarily pressing Flamel to come and dine, felt the full irony of the situation. To use Flamel as a shield against his wife's scrutiny was only a shade less humiliating than to reckon on his wife as a defence against Flamel.

He felt a contradictory movement of annoyance at the latter's ready acceptance, and the two men drove in silence to the station. As they passed the bookstall in the waiting room, Flamel lingered a moment and the eyes of both fell on Margaret Aubyn's name, conspicuously displayed above a counter stacked with the familiar volumes.

'We shall be late, you know,' Glennard remonstrated, pulling out his watch.

'Go ahead,' said Flamel, imperturbably. 'I want to get something –'

Glennard turned on his heel and walked down the platform. Flamel rejoined him with an innocent-looking magazine in his hand; but Glennard dared not even glance at the cover, lest it should show the syllables he feared.

The train was full of people they knew, and they were kept apart till it dropped them at the little suburban station. As they strolled up the shaded hill, Glennard talked volubly, pointing out the improvements in the neighbourhood, deploring the threatened approach of an electric railway, and screening himself by a series of reflex adjustments from the risk of any allusion to the *Letters*. Flamel suffered his discourse with the bland inattention that we accord to the affairs of someone else's suburb, and they reached the shelter of Alexa's tea table without a perceptible turn toward the dreaded topic.

The dinner passed off safely. Flamel, always at his best in Alexa's presence, gave her the kind of attention which is like a becoming light thrown on the speaker's words: his answers seemed to bring out a latent significance in her phrases, as the sculptor draws his statue from the block. Glennard, under his wife's composure, detected a sensibility to this manoeuvre, and the discovery was like the lightning flash across a nocturnal landscape. Thus far these momentary illuminations had served only to reveal the strangeness of the intervening country: each fresh observation seemed to increase the sum total of his ignorance. Her simplicity of outline was more puzzling than a complex surface. One may conceivably work one's way through a labyrinth; but Alexa's candour was like a snow-covered plain where, the road once lost, there are no landmarks to travel by.

Dinner over, they returned to the veranda, where a moon, rising behind the old elm, was combining with that complaisant tree a romantic enlargement of their borders. Glennard had forgotten the cigars. He went to his study to fetch them, and in passing through the drawing room he saw the second volume of the *Letters* lying open on his wife's table. He picked up the book and looked at the date of the letter she had been reading. It was one of the last... he knew the few lines by heart. He dropped the book and leant against the wall. Why had he included that one among the others? Or was it possible that now they would all seem like that?...

Alexa's voice came suddenly out of the dusk. 'May Touchett was right – it *is* like listening at a keyhole. I wish I hadn't read it!'

Flamel returned, in the leisurely tone of the man whose

phrases are punctuated by a cigarette, 'It seems so to us, perhaps; but to another generation the book will be a classic.'

'Then it ought not to have been published till it had time to become a classic. It's horrible, it's degrading almost, to read the secrets of a woman one might have known.' She added, in a lower tone, 'Stephen *did* know her –'

'Did he?' came from Flamel.

'He knew her very well, at Hillbridge, years ago. The book has made him feel dreadfully… he wouldn't read it… he didn't want me to read it. I didn't understand at first, but now I can see how horribly disloyal it must seem to him. It's so much worse to surprise a friend's secrets than a stranger's.'

'Oh, Glennard's such a sensitive chap,' Flamel said, easily; and Alexa almost rebukingly rejoined, 'If you'd known her I'm sure you'd feel as he does…'

Glennard stood motionless, overcome by the singular infelicity with which he had contrived to put Flamel in possession of the two points most damaging to his case: the fact that he had been a friend of Margaret Aubyn's, and that he had concealed from Alexa his share in the publication of the letters. To a man of less than Flamel's astuteness it must now be clear to whom the letters were addressed; and the possibility once suggested, nothing could be easier than to confirm it by discreet research. An impulse of self-accusal drove Glennard to the window. Why not anticipate betrayal by telling his wife the truth in Flamel's presence? If the man had a drop of decent feeling in him, such a course would be the surest means of securing his silence; and above all, it would rid Glennard of the necessity of defending himself against the perpetual criticism of his wife's belief in him…

The impulse was strong enough to carry him to the window; but there a reaction of defiance set in. What had he done, after all, to need defence and explanation? Both Dresham and Flamel had, in his hearing, declared the publication of the letters to be not only justifiable but obligatory; and if the disinterestedness of Flamel's verdict might be questioned, Dresham's at least represented the impartial view of the man of letters. As to Alexa's words, they were simply the conventional utterance of the 'nice' woman on a question already decided for her by other 'nice' women. She had said the proper thing as mechanically as she would have put on the appropriate gown or written the correct form of dinner invitation. Glennard had small faith in the abstract judgements of the other sex; he knew that half the women who were horrified by the publication of Mrs Aubyn's letters would have betrayed her secrets without a scruple.

The sudden lowering of his emotional pitch brought a proportionate relief. He told himself that now the worst was over and things would fall into perspective again. His wife and Flamel had turned to other topics, and coming out on the veranda, he handed the cigars to Flamel, saying, cheerfully – and yet he could have sworn they were the last words he meant to utter! – 'Look here, old man, before you go down to Newport you must come out and spend a few days with us – mustn't he, Alexa?'

8

Glennard, perhaps unconsciously, had counted on the continuance of this easier mood. He had always taken pride in a certain robustness of fibre that enabled him to harden himself against the inevitable, to convert his failures into the building materials of success. Though it did not even now occur to him that what he called the inevitable had hitherto been the alternative he happened to prefer, he was yet obscurely aware that his present difficulty was one not to be conjured by any affectation of indifference. Some griefs build the soul a spacious house, but in this misery of Glennard's he could not stand upright. It pressed against him at every turn. He told himself that this was because there was no escape from the visible evidences of his act. The *Letters* confronted him everywhere. People who had never opened a book discussed them with critical reservations; to have read them had become a social obligation in circles to which literature never penetrates except in a personal guise.

Glennard did himself injustice. It was from the unexpected discovery of his own pettiness that he chiefly suffered. Our self-esteem is apt to be based on the hypothetical great act we have never had occasion to perform; and even the most self-scrutinising modesty credits itself negatively with a high standard of conduct. Glennard had never thought himself a hero; but he had been certain that he was incapable of baseness. We all like our wrongdoings to have a becoming cut, to be made to order, as it were; and Glennard found himself suddenly thrust into a garb of dishonour surely meant for a meaner figure.

The immediate result of his first weeks of wretchedness was the resolve to go to town for the winter. He knew that such a course was just beyond the limit of prudence; but it was easy to allay the fears of Alexa who, scrupulously vigilant in the management of the household, preserved the American wife's usual aloofness from her husband's business cares. Glennard felt that he could not trust himself to a winter's solitude with her. He had an unspeakable dread of her learning the truth about the letters, yet could not be sure of steeling himself against the suicidal impulse of avowal. His very soul was parched for sympathy; he thirsted for a voice of pity and comprehension. But would his wife pity? Would she understand? Again he found himself brought up abruptly against his incredible ignorance of her nature. The fact that he knew well enough how she would behave in the ordinary emergencies of life, that he could count, in such contingencies, on the kind of high courage and directness he had always divined in her, made him the more hopeless of her entering into the tortuous psychology of an act that he himself could no longer explain or understand. It would have been easier had she been more complex, more feminine – if he could have counted on her imaginative sympathy or her moral obtuseness – but he was sure of neither. He was sure of nothing but that, for a time, he must avoid her. Glennard could not rid himself of the delusion that, by and by, his action would cease to make its consequences felt. He would not have cared to own to himself that he counted on the dulling of his sensibilities: he preferred to indulge the vague hypothesis that extraneous circumstances would somehow efface the blot upon his conscience. In his worst moments of self-abasement he tried to find solace in the thought that Flamel had sanctioned his course. Flamel, at the outset, must have guessed to whom the letters were addressed; yet neither then nor afterwards had he hesitated to advise their publication. This thought drew Glennard to him in fitful impulses of friendliness, from each of which there was a sharper reaction of distrust and aversion. When Flamel was not at the house, he missed the support of his tacit connivance; when he was there, his presence seemed the assertion of an intolerable claim.

Early in the winter the Glennards took possession of the

little house that was to cost them almost nothing. The change brought Glennard the relief of seeing less of his wife, and of being protected, in her presence, by the multiplied preoccupations of town life. Alexa, who could never appear hurried, showed the smiling abstraction of a pretty woman to whom the social side of married life has not lost its novelty. Glennard, with the recklessness of a man fresh from his first financial imprudence, encouraged her in such little extravagances as her good sense at first resisted. Since they had come to town, he argued, they might as well enjoy themselves. He took a sympathetic view of the necessity of new gowns, he gave her a set of furs at Christmas, and before the New Year they had agreed on the obligation of adding a parlourmaid to their small establishment.

Providence the very next day hastened to justify this measure by placing on Glennard's breakfast plate an envelope bearing the name of the publishers to whom he had sold Mrs Aubyn's letters. It happened to be the only letter the early post had brought, and he glanced across the table at his wife, who had come down before him and had probably laid the envelope on his plate. She was not the woman to ask awkward questions, but he felt the conjecture of her glance, and he was debating whether to affect surprise at the receipt of the letter, or to pass it off as a business communication that had strayed to his house, when a cheque fell from the envelope. It was the royalty on the first edition of the letters. His first feeling was one of simple satisfaction. The money had come with such infernal opportuneness that he could not help welcoming it. Before long, too, there would be more; he knew the book was still selling far beyond the publisher's previsions. He put the cheque in his pocket and left the room without looking at his wife.

On the way to his office the habitual reaction set in. The money he had received was the first tangible reminder that he was living on the sale of his self-esteem. The thought of material benefit had been overshadowed by his sense of the intrinsic baseness of making the letters known; now he saw what an element of sordidness it added to the situation and how the fact that he needed the money, and must use it, pledged him more irrevocably than ever to the consequences of his act. It seemed to him, in that first hour of misery, that he had betrayed his friend anew.

When, that afternoon, he reached home earlier than usual, Alexa's drawing room was full of a gaiety that overflowed to the stairs. Flamel, for a wonder, was not there; but Dresham and young Hartly, grouped about the tea table, were receiving with resonant mirth a narrative delivered in the fluttered staccato that made Mrs Armiger's conversation like the ejaculations of a startled aviary.

She paused as Glennard entered, and he had time to notice that his wife, who was busied about the tea tray, had not joined in the laughter of the men.

'Oh, go on, go on,' young Hartly rapturously groaned; and Mrs Armiger met Glennard's enquiry with the deprecating cry that really she didn't see what there was to laugh at. 'I'm sure I feel more like crying. I don't know what I should have done if Alexa hadn't been home to give me a cup of tea. My nerves are in shreds – yes, another, dear, please –' and as Glennard looked his perplexity, she went on, after pondering on the selection of a second lump of sugar, 'Why, I've just come from the reading, you know – the reading at the Waldorf.'

'I haven't been in town long enough to know anything,' said Glennard, taking the cup his wife handed him. 'Who has been reading what?'

57

'That lovely girl from the South – Georgie – Georgie What's-her-name – Mrs Dresham's protégée – unless she's *yours*, Mr Dresham! Why, the big ballroom was *packed*, and all the women were crying like idiots – it was the most harrowing thing I ever heard –'

'What *did* you hear?' Glennard asked, and his wife interposed: 'Won't you have another bit of cake, Julia? Or, Stephen, ring for some hot toast, please.' Her tone betrayed a polite weariness of the topic under discussion. Glennard turned to the bell, but Mrs Armiger pursued him with her lovely amazement.

'Why, the *Aubyn Letters* – didn't you know about it? She read them so beautifully that it was quite horrible – I should have fainted if there'd been a man near enough to carry me out.'

Hartly's glee redoubled, and Dresham said jovially, 'How like you women to raise a shriek over the book and then do all you can to encourage the blatant publicity of the readings!'

Mrs Armiger met him more than halfway on a torrent of self-accusal. 'It *was* horrid; it was disgraceful. I told your wife we ought all to be ashamed of ourselves for going, and I think Alexa was quite right to refuse to take any tickets – even if it was for a charity.'

'Oh,' her hostess murmured, indifferently, 'with me charity begins at home. I can't afford emotional luxuries.'

'A charity? A charity?' Hartly exulted. 'I hadn't seized the full beauty of it. Reading poor Margaret Aubyn's love letters at the Waldorf before five hundred people for a charity! *What* charity, dear Mrs Armiger?'

'Why, the Home for Friendless Women –'

'It was well chosen,' Dresham commented; and Hartly buried his mirth in the sofa cushions.

When they were alone Glennard, still holding his untouched cup of tea, turned to his wife, who sat silently behind the kettle. 'Who asked you to take a ticket for that reading?'

'I don't know, really – Kate Dresham, I fancy. It was she who got it up.'

'It's just the sort of damnable vulgarity she's capable of! It's loathsome – it's monstrous –'

His wife, without looking up, answered gravely, 'I thought so too. It was for that reason I didn't go. But you must remember that very few people feel about Mrs Aubyn as you do –'

Glennard managed to set down his cup with a steady hand, but the room swung round with him and he dropped into the nearest chair. 'As I do?' he repeated.

'I mean that very few people knew her when she lived in New York. To most of the women who went to the reading she was a mere name, too remote to have any personality. With me, of course, it was different –'

Glennard gave her a startled look. 'Different? Why different?'

'Since you were her friend –'

'Her friend!' He stood up impatiently. 'You speak as if she had had only one – the most famous woman of her day!' He moved vaguely about the room, bending down to look at some books on the table. 'I hope,' he added, 'you didn't give that as a reason, by the way?'

'A reason?'

'For not going. A woman who gives reasons for getting out of social obligations is sure to make herself unpopular or ridiculous.'

The words were uncalculated; but in an instant he saw that they had strangely bridged the distance between his wife and

59

himself. He felt her close on him, like a panting foe; and her answer was a flash that showed the hand on the trigger.

'I seem,' she said from the threshold, 'to have done both in giving my reason to you.'

The fact that they were dining out that evening made it easy for him to avoid Alexa till she came downstairs in her opera-cloak. Mrs Touchett, who was going to the same dinner, had offered to call for her, and Glennard, refusing a precarious seat between the ladies' draperies, followed on foot. The evening was interminable. The reading at the Waldorf, at which all the women had been present, had revived the discussion of the *Aubyn Letters*, and Glennard, hearing his wife questioned as to her absence, felt himself miserably wishing that she had gone, rather than that her staying away should have been remarked. He was rapidly losing all sense of proportion where the *Letters* were concerned. He could no longer hear them mentioned without suspecting a purpose in the allusion; he even yielded himself for a moment to the extravagance of imagining that Mrs Dresham, whom he disliked, had organised the reading in the hope of making him betray himself – for he was already sure that Dresham had divined his share in the transaction.

The attempt to keep a smooth surface on this inner tumult was as endless and unavailing as efforts made in a nightmare. He lost all sense of what he was saying to his neighbours; and once, when he looked up, his wife's glance struck him cold.

She sat nearly opposite him, at Flamel's side, and it appeared to Glennard that they had built about themselves one of those airy barriers of talk behind which two people can say what they please. While the reading was discussed they were silent. Their silence seemed to Glennard almost cynical –

it stripped the last disguise from their complicity. A throb of anger rose in him, but suddenly it fell, and he felt, with a curious sense of relief, that at bottom he no longer cared whether Flamel had told his wife or not. The assumption that Flamel knew about the letters had become a fact to Glennard; and it now seemed to him better that Alexa should know too.

He was frightened at first by the discovery of his own indifference. The last barriers of his will seemed to be breaking down before a flood of moral lassitude. How could he continue to play his part, how keep his front to the enemy, with this poison of indifference stealing through his veins? He tried to brace himself with the remembrance of his wife's scorn. He had not forgotten the note on which their conversation had closed. If he had ever wondered how she would receive the truth he wondered no longer – she would despise him. But this lent a new insidiousness to his temptation, since her contempt would be a refuge from his own. He said to himself that, since he no longer cared for the consequences, he could at least acquit himself of speaking in self-defence. What he wanted now was not immunity but castigation: his wife's indignation might still reconcile him to himself. Therein lay his one hope of regeneration; her scorn was the moral antiseptic that he needed, her comprehension the one balm that could heal him…

When they left the dinner he was so afraid of speaking that he let her drive home alone, and went to the club with Flamel.

9

He rose next morning with the resolve to know what Alexa thought of him. It was not anchoring in a haven, but lying to in a storm – he felt the need of a temporary lull in the turmoil of his sensations.

He came home late, for they were dining alone and he knew that they would have the evening together. When he followed her to the drawing room after dinner he thought himself on the point of speaking; but as she handed him his coffee he said, involuntarily: 'I shall have to carry this off to the study, I've got a lot of work tonight.'

Alone in the study he cursed his cowardice. What was it that had withheld him? A certain bright unapproachableness seemed to keep him at arm's length. She was not the kind of woman whose compassion could be circumvented; there was no chance of slipping past the outposts; he would never take her by surprise. Well – why not face her, then? What he shrank from could be no worse than what he was enduring. He had pushed back his chair and turned to go upstairs when a new expedient presented itself. What if, instead of telling her, he were to let her find out for herself, and watch the effect of the discovery before speaking? In this way he made over to chance the burden of the revelation.

The idea had been suggested by the sight of the formula enclosing the publisher's cheque. He had deposited the money, but the notice accompanying it dropped from his notecase as he cleared his table for work. It was the formula usual in such cases, and revealed clearly enough that he was the recipient of a royalty on Margaret Aubyn's letters. It would be impossible for Alexa to read it without understanding at once that the letters had been written to him and that he had sold them…

He sat downstairs till he heard her ring for the parlourmaid to put out the lights; then he went up to the drawing room with a bundle of papers in his hand. Alexa was just rising from her seat and the lamplight fell on the deep roll of hair that overhung her brow like the eaves of a temple. Her face had often the high secluded look of a shrine; and it was this touch of awe in her beauty that now made him feel himself on the brink of sacrilege.

Lest the feeling should control him, he spoke at once. 'I've brought you a piece of work – a lot of old bills and things that I want you to sort for me. Some are not worth keeping – but you'll be able to judge of that. There may be a letter or two among them – nothing of much account, but I don't like to throw away the whole lot without having them looked over and I haven't time to do it myself.'

He held out the papers and she took them with a smile that seemed to recognise in the service he asked the tacit intention of making amends for the incident of the previous day.

'Are you sure I shall know which to keep?'

'Oh, quite sure,' he answered, easily – 'and besides, none are of much importance.'

The next morning he invented an excuse for leaving the house without seeing her, and when he returned, just before dinner, he found a visitor's hat and stick in the hall. The visitor was Flamel, who was in the act of taking leave.

He had risen, but Alexa remained seated; and their attitude gave the impression of a colloquy that had prolonged itself beyond the limits of speech. Both turned a surprised eye on Glennard, and he had the sense of walking into a room grown suddenly empty, as though their thoughts were conspirators dispersed by his approach. He felt the clutch of his old fear. What if his wife had already sorted the papers and had told Flamel of her discovery? Well, it was no news to Flamel that Glennard was in receipt of a royalty on the *Aubyn Letters*...

A sudden resolve to know the worst made him lift his eyes

to his wife as the door closed on Flamel. But Alexa had risen also, and bending over her writing table, with her back to Glennard, was beginning to speak precipitately.

'I'm dining out tonight – you don't mind my deserting you? Julia Armiger sent me word just now that she had an extra ticket for the last Ambrose concert. She told me to say how sorry she was that she hadn't two – but I knew *you* wouldn't be sorry!' She ended with a laugh that had the effect of being a strayed echo of Mrs Armiger's; and before Glennard could speak she had added, with her hand on the door, 'Mr Flamel stayed so late that I've hardly time to dress. The concert begins ridiculously early, and Julia dines at half-past seven –'

Glennard stood alone in the empty room that seemed somehow full of an ironical consciousness of what was happening. 'She hates me,' he murmured. 'She hates me…'

The next day was Sunday, and Glennard purposely lingered late in his room. When he came downstairs his wife was already seated at the breakfast table. She lifted her usual smile to his entrance and they took shelter in the nearest topic, like wayfarers overtaken by a storm. While he listened to her account of the concert he began to think that, after all, she had not yet sorted the papers, and that her agitation of the previous day must be ascribed to another cause, in which perhaps he had but an indirect concern. He wondered it had never before occurred to him that Flamel was the kind of man who might very well please a woman at his own expense, without need of fortuitous assistance. If this possibility cleared the outlook it did not brighten it. Glennard merely felt himself left alone with his baseness.

Alexa left the breakfast table before him and when he went up to the drawing room he found her dressed to go out.

'Aren't you a little early for church?' he asked.

She replied that, on the way there, she meant to stop a moment at her mother's; and while she drew on her gloves, he fumbled among the knick-knacks on the mantelpiece for a match to light his cigarette.

'Well, goodbye,' she said, turning to go; and from the threshold she added: 'By the way, I've sorted the papers you gave me. Those that I thought you would like to keep are on your study table.' She went downstairs and he heard the door close behind her.

She had sorted the papers – she knew, then – she *must* know – and she had made no sign!

Glennard, he hardly knew how, found himself once more in the study. On the table lay the packet he had given her. It was much smaller – she had evidently gone over the papers with care, destroying the greater number. He loosened the elastic band and spread the remaining envelopes on his desk. The publisher's notice was among them.

10

His wife knew and she made no sign. Glennard found himself in the case of the seafarer who, closing his eyes at nightfall on a scene he thinks to put leagues behind him before day, wakes to a porthole framing the same patch of shore. From the kind of exaltation to which his resolve had lifted him he dropped to an unreasoning apathy. His impulse of confession had acted as a drug to self-reproach. He had tried to shift a portion of his burden to his wife's shoulders; and now that she had tacitly refused to carry it, he felt the load too heavy to be taken up again.

A fortunate interval of hard work brought respite from this phase of sterile misery. He went West to argue an important case, won it, and came back to fresh preoccupations. His own affairs were thriving enough to engross him in the pauses of his professional work, and for over two months he had little time to look himself in the face. Not unnaturally – for he was as yet unskilled in the subtleties of introspection – he mistook his temporary insensibility for a gradual revival of moral health.

He told himself that he was recovering his sense of proportion, getting to see things in their true light; and if he now thought of his rash appeal to his wife's sympathy it was as an act of folly from the consequences of which he had been saved by the providence that watches over madmen. He had little leisure to observe Alexa; but he concluded that the common sense momentarily denied him had counselled her silent acceptance of the inevitable. If such a quality was a poor substitute for the passionate justness that had once seemed to distinguish her, he accepted the alternative as a part of that general lowering of the key that seems needful to the maintenance of the matrimonial duet. What woman ever retained her abstract sense of justice where another woman was concerned? Possibly the thought that he had profited by Mrs Aubyn's tenderness was not wholly disagreeable to his wife.

When the pressure of work began to lessen, and he found himself, in the lengthening afternoons, able to reach home somewhat earlier, he noticed that the little drawing room was always full and that he and his wife seldom had an evening alone together. When he was tired, as often happened, she went out alone; the idea of giving up an engagement to remain with him seemed not to occur to her. She had shown, as a girl, little fondness for society, nor had she seemed to regret it during the year they had spent in the country. He reflected, however, that he was sharing the common lot of husbands, who proverbially mistake the early ardours of housekeeping for a sign of settled domesticity. Alexa, at any rate, was refuting his theory as inconsiderately as a seedling defeats the gardener's expectations. An indefinable change had come over her. In one sense it was a happy one, since she had grown, if not handsomer, at least more vivid and expressive; her beauty had become more communicable: it was as though she had learnt the conscious exercise of intuitive attributes and now used her effects with the discrimination of an artist skilled in values. To a dispassionate critic (as Glennard now rated himself) the art may at times have been a little too obvious. Her attempts at lightness lacked spontaneity, and she sometimes rasped him by laughing like Julia Armiger; but he had enough imagination to perceive that, in respect of his wife's social arts, a husband necessarily sees the wrong side of the tapestry.

In this ironical estimate of their relation Glennard found himself strangely relieved of all concern as to his wife's feelings for Flamel. From an Olympian pinnacle of indifference he calmly surveyed their inoffensive antics. It was surprising how his cheapening of his wife put him at ease with himself. Far as he and she were from each other they yet had, in a sense, the tacit nearness of complicity. Yes, they were accomplices; he could no more be jealous of her than she could despise him. The jealousy that would once have seemed a blur on her whiteness now appeared like a tribute to ideals in which he no longer believed.

Glennard was little given to exploring the outskirts of literature. He always skipped the 'literary notices' in the papers, and he had small leisure for the intermittent pleasures of the periodical. He had therefore no notion of the prolonged reverberations which the *Aubyn Letters* had awakened. When the book ceased to be talked about he supposed it had ceased to be read; and this apparent subsidence of the agitation about it brought the reassuring sense that he had exaggerated its vitality. The conviction, if it did not ease his conscience, at least offered him the relative relief of obscurity; he felt like an offender taken down from the pillory and thrust into the soothing darkness of a cell.

But one evening, when Alexa had left him to go to a dance, he chanced to turn over the magazines on her table, and the copy of the *Horoscope*, to which he settled down with his cigar, confronted him, on its first page, with a portrait of Margaret Aubyn. It was a reproduction of the photograph that had stood so long on his desk. The desiccating air of memory had turned her into the mere abstraction of a woman, and this unexpected evocation seemed to bring her nearer than she had ever been in life. Was it because he understood her better? He looked long into her eyes; little personal traits reached out to him like caresses – the tired droop of her lids, her quick way of leaning forward as she spoke, the movements of her long expressive hands. All that was feminine in her, the quality he had always missed, stole towards him from her unreproachful gaze; and now that it was too late, life had developed in him the subtler perceptions which could detect it in even this poor semblance of herself. For a moment he found consolation in the thought that, at any cost, they had thus been brought together; then a flood of shame rushed over him. Face to face with her, he felt himself laid bare to the inmost fold of consciousness. The shame was deep, but it was a renovating anguish: he was like a man whom intolerable pain has roused from the creeping lethargy of death…

He rose next morning to as fresh a sense of life as though his hour of mute communion with Margaret Aubyn had been a more exquisite renewal of their earlier meetings. His waking thought was that he must see her again; and as consciousness affirmed itself he felt an intense fear of losing the sense of her nearness. But she was still close to him: her presence remained the one reality in a world of shadows. All through his working hours he was reliving with incredible minuteness every incident of their obliterated past; as a man who has mastered the spirit of a foreign tongue turns with renewed wonder to the pages his youth has plodded over. In this lucidity of retrospection the most trivial detail had its meaning, and the joy of recovery was embittered to Glennard by the perception of all that he had missed. He had been pitiably, grotesquely stupid; and there was irony in the thought that, but for the crisis through which he was passing, he might have lived on in complacent ignorance of his loss. It was as though she had bought him with her blood…

That evening he and Alexa dined alone. After dinner he followed her to the drawing room. He no longer felt the need of avoiding her; he was hardly conscious of her presence. After a few words they lapsed into silence, and he sat smoking with his eyes on the fire. It was not that he was unwilling to talk to her; he felt a curious desire to be as kind as possible; but he was always forgetting that she was there. Her full bright presence, through which the currents of life flowed so warmly, had grown as tenuous as a shadow, and he saw so far beyond her.

Presently she rose and began to move about the room. She

seemed to be looking for something, and he roused himself to ask what she wanted.

'Only the last number of the *Horoscope*. I thought I'd left it on this table.' He said nothing, and she went on: 'You haven't seen it?'

'No,' he returned coldly. The magazine was locked in his desk.

His wife had moved to the mantelpiece. She stood facing him, and as he looked up he met her tentative gaze. 'I was reading an article in it – a review of Mrs Aubyn's *Letters*,' she added, slowly, with her deep, deliberate blush.

Glennard stooped to toss his cigar into the fire. He felt a savage wish that she would not speak the other woman's name; nothing else seemed to matter.

'You seem to do a lot of reading,' he said.

She still earnestly confronted him. 'I was keeping this for you – I thought it might interest you,' she said, with an air of gentle insistence.

He stood up and turned away. He was sure she knew that he had taken the review, and he felt that he was beginning to hate her again.

'I haven't time for such things,' he said, indifferently. As he moved to the door he heard her take a hurried step forward; then she paused, and sank without speaking into the chair from which he had risen.

11

As Glennard, in the raw February sunlight, mounted the road to the cemetery, he felt the beatitude that comes with an abrupt cessation of physical pain. He had reached the point where self-analysis ceases; the impulse that moved him was purely intuitive. He did not even seek a reason for it, beyond the obvious one that his desire to stand by Margaret Aubyn's grave was prompted by no attempt at a sentimental reparation, but rather by the need to affirm in some way the reality of the tie between them.

The ironical promiscuity of death had brought Mrs Aubyn back to share the hospitality of her husband's last lodging; but though Glennard knew she had been buried near New York he had never visited her grave. He was oppressed, as he now threaded the long avenues, by a chilling vision of her return. There was no family to follow her hearse; she had died alone, as she had lived; and the 'distinguished mourners' who had formed the escort of the famous writer knew nothing of the woman they were committing to the grave. Glennard could not even remember at what season she had been buried; but his mood indulged the fancy that it must have been on some such day of harsh sunlight, the incisive February brightness that gives perspicuity without warmth. The white avenues stretched before him interminably, lined with stereotyped emblems of affliction, as though all the platitudes ever uttered had been turned to marble and set up over the unresisting dead. Here and there, no doubt, a frigid urn or an insipid angel imprisoned some fine-fibred grief, as the most hackneyed words may become the vehicle of rare meanings; but for the most part the endless alignment of monuments seemed to embody those easy generalisations about death that do not disturb the repose of the living. Glennard's eye, as he followed the way pointed out to him, had instinctively sought some low mound with a quiet headstone. He had forgotten that the dead seldom plan their own houses, and with a pang he discovered the name he sought on the cyclopean base of a shaft rearing its aggressive height at the angle of two avenues.

'How she would have hated it!' he murmured.

A bench stood near and he seated himself. The monument rose before him like some pretentious uninhabited dwelling; he could not believe that Margaret Aubyn lay there. It was a Sunday morning, and black figures moved among the paths, placing flowers on the frost-bound hillocks. Glennard noticed that the neighbouring graves had been thus newly dressed; and he fancied a blind stir of expectancy through the sod, as though the bare mounds spread a parched surface to that commemorative rain. He rose presently and walked back to the entrance of the cemetery. Several greenhouses stood near the gates, and turning in at the first he asked for some flowers.

'Anything in the emblematic line?' asked the anaemic man behind the dripping counter.

Glennard shook his head.

'Just cut flowers? This way, then.' The florist unlocked a glass door and led him down a moist green aisle. The hot air was choked with the scent of white azaleas, white lilies, white lilacs; all the flowers were white; they were like a prolongation, a mystical efflorescence, of the long rows of marble tombstones, and their perfume seemed to cover an odour of decay. The rich atmosphere made Glennard dizzy. As he leaned in the doorway, waiting for the flowers, he had a penetrating sense of Margaret Aubyn's nearness – not the imponderable presence of his inner vision, but a life that beat warm in his arms…

The sharp air caught him as he stepped out into it again. He walked back and scattered the flowers over the grave. The edges of the white petals shrivelled like burnt paper in the cold; and as he watched them, the illusion of her nearness faded, shrank back, frozen.

12

The motive of his visit to the cemetery remained undefined save as a final effort of escape from his wife's inexpressive acceptance of his shame. It seemed to him that as long as he could keep himself alive to that shame he would not wholly have succumbed to its consequences. His chief fear was that he should become the creature of his act. His wife's indifference degraded him: it seemed to put him on a level with his dishonour. Margaret Aubyn would have abhorred the deed in proportion to her pity for the man. The sense of her potential pity drew him back to her. The one woman knew but did not understand; the other, it sometimes seemed, understood without knowing.

In its last disguise of retrospective remorse, his self-pity affected a desire for solitude and meditation. He lost himself in morbid musings, in futile visions of what life with Margaret Aubyn might have been. There were moments when, in the strange dislocation of his view, the wrong he had done her seemed a tie between them.

To indulge these emotions he fell into the habit, on Sunday afternoons, of solitary walks prolonged till after dusk. The days were lengthening, there was a touch of spring in the air, and his wanderings now usually led him to the park and its outlying regions.

One Sunday, tired of aimless locomotion, he took a cab at the park gates and let it carry him out to the Riverside Drive. It was a grey afternoon streaked with east wind. Glennard's cab advanced slowly, and as he leant back, gazing with absent intentness at the deserted paths that wound under bare boughs between grass banks of premature vividness, his attention was arrested by two figures walking ahead of him.

This couple, who had the path to themselves, moved at an uneven pace, as though adapting their gait to a conversation marked by meditative intervals. Now and then they paused, and in one of these pauses the lady, turning towards her companion, showed Glennard the outline of his wife's profile. The man was Flamel.

The blood rushed to Glennard's forehead. He sat up with a jerk and pushed back the lid in the roof of the hansom; but when the cabman bent down he dropped into his seat without speaking. Then, becoming conscious of the prolonged interrogation of the lifted lid, he called out, 'Turn – drive back – anywhere – I'm in a hurry –'

As the cab swung round he caught a last glimpse of the two figures. They had not moved; Alexa, with bent head, stood listening.

'My God, my God –' he groaned.

It was hideous – it was abominable – he could not understand it. The woman was nothing to him – less than nothing – yet the blood hummed in his ears and hung a cloud before him. He knew it was only the stirring of the primal instinct, that it had no more to do with his reasoning self than any reflex impulse of the body; but that merely lowered anguish to disgust. Yes, it was disgust he felt – almost a physical nausea. The poisonous fumes of life were in his lungs. He was sick, unutterably sick...

He drove home and went to his room. They were giving a little dinner that night, and when he came down the guests were arriving. He looked at his wife: her beauty was extraordinary, but it seemed to him the beauty of a smooth sea along an unlit coast. She frightened him.

He sat late in his study. He heard the parlourmaid lock the front door; then his wife went upstairs and the lights were put out. His brain was like some great empty hall with an echo in it: one thought reverberated endlessly... At length he drew his chair to the table and began to write. He addressed an envelope and then slowly reread what he had written.

My dear Flamel,
Many apologies for not sending you sooner the enclosed
cheque, which represents the customary percentage on the
sale of the Letters.
Trusting you will excuse the oversight,
Yours truly,

– Stephen Glennard

He let himself out of the darkened house and dropped the letter in the postbox at the corner.

The next afternoon he was detained late at his office, and as he was preparing to leave he heard someone asking for him in the outer room. He seated himself again and Flamel was shown in.

The two men, as Glennard pushed aside an obstructive chair, had a moment to measure each other; then Flamel advanced, and drawing out his notecase, laid a slip of paper on the desk.

'My dear fellow, what on earth does this mean?'

Glennard recognised his cheque.

'That I was remiss, simply. It ought to have gone to you before.'

Flamel's tone had been that of unaffected surprise, but at this his accent changed and he asked quickly: 'On what ground?'

Glennard had moved away from the desk and stood leaning against the calf-backed volumes of the bookcase. 'On the ground that you sold Mrs Aubyn's letters for me, and that

I find the intermediary in such cases is entitled to a percentage on the sale.'

Flamel paused before answering. 'You find, you say. It's a recent discovery?'

'Obviously, from my not sending the cheque sooner. You see, I'm new to the business.'

'And since when have you discovered that there was any question of business, as far as I was concerned?'

Glennard flushed and his voice rose slightly. 'Are you reproaching me for not having remembered it sooner?'

Flamel, who had spoken in the rapid repressed tone of a man on the verge of anger, stared a moment at this and then, in his natural voice, rejoined, good-humouredly, 'Upon my soul, I don't understand you!'

The change of key seemed to disconcert Glennard. 'It's simple enough,' he muttered.

'Simple enough – your offering me money in return for a friendly service? I don't know what your other friends expect!'

'Some of my friends wouldn't have undertaken the job. Those who would have done so would probably have expected to be paid.'

He lifted his eyes to Flamel and the two men looked at each other. Flamel had turned white and his lips stirred, but he held his temperate note. 'If you mean to imply that the job was not a nice one, you lay yourself open to the retort that you proposed it. But for my part I've never seen, I never shall see, any reason for not publishing the letters.'

'That's just it!'

'What –?'

'The certainty of your not seeing was what made me go to you. When a man's got stolen goods to pawn he doesn't take them to the police station.'

76

'Stolen?' Flamel echoed. 'The letters were stolen?'

Glennard burst into a laugh. 'How much longer do you expect me to keep up that pretence about the letters? You knew well enough they were written to me.'

Flamel looked at him in silence. 'Were they?' he said at length. 'I didn't know it.'

'And didn't suspect it, I suppose,' Glennard sneered.

The other was again silent; then he said, 'I may remind you that, supposing I had felt any curiosity about the matter, I had no way of finding out that the letters were written to you. You never showed me the originals.'

'What does that prove? There were fifty ways of finding out. It's the kind of thing one can easily do.'

Flamel glanced at him with contempt. 'Our ideas probably differ as to what a man can easily do. It would not have been easy for me.'

Glennard's anger vented itself in the words uppermost in his thought. 'It may, then, interest you to hear that my wife *does* know about the letters – has known for some months…'

'Ah,' said the other, slowly.

Glennard saw that, in his blind clutch at a weapon, he had seized the one most apt to wound. Flamel's muscles were under control, but his face showed the indefinable change produced by the slow infiltration of poison. Every implication that the words contained had reached its mark; but Glennard felt that their obvious intent was lost in the anguish of what they suggested. He was sure now that Flamel would never have betrayed him; but the inference only made a wider outlet for his anger. He paused breathlessly for Flamel to speak.

'If she knows, it's not through me.' It was what Glennard had waited for.

'Through you, by God? Who said it was through you? Do you suppose I leave it to you, or to anybody else, for that matter, to keep my wife informed of my actions? I didn't suppose even such egregious conceit as yours could delude a man to that degree!' Struggling for a foothold in the small landslide of his dignity, he added, in a steadier tone, 'My wife learnt the facts from me.'

Flamel received this in silence. The other's outbreak seemed to have restored his self-control, and when he spoke it was with a deliberation implying that his course was chosen. 'In that case I understand still less –'

'Still less –?'

'The meaning of this.' He pointed to the cheque. 'When you began to speak I supposed you had meant it as a bribe; now I can only infer it was intended as a random insult. In either case, here's my answer.'

He tore the slip of paper in two and tossed the fragments across the desk to Glennard. Then he turned and walked out of the office.

Glennard dropped his head on his hands. If he had hoped to restore his self-respect by the simple expedient of assailing Flamel's, the result had not justified his expectation. The blow he had struck had blunted the edge of his anger, and the unforeseen extent of the hurt inflicted did not alter the fact that his weapon had broken in his hands. He saw now that his rage against Flamel was only the last projection of a passionate self-disgust. This consciousness did not dull his dislike of the man; it simply made reprisals ineffectual. Flamel's unwillingness to quarrel with him was the last stage of his abasement.

In the light of this final humiliation his assumption of his wife's indifference struck him as hardly so fatuous as the sentimental resuscitation of his past. He had been living in a factitious world wherein his emotions were the sycophants of his vanity, and it was with instinctive relief that he felt its ruins crash about his head.

It was nearly dark when he left his office, and he walked slowly homeward in the complete mental abeyance that follows on such a crisis. He was not aware that he was thinking of his wife; yet when he reached his own door he found that, in the involuntary readjustment of his vision, she had once more become the central point of consciousness.

13

It had never before occurred to him that she might, after all, have missed the purport of the document he had put in her way. What if, in her hurried inspection of the papers, she had passed it over as related to the private business of some client? What, for instance, was to prevent her concluding that Glennard was the counsel of the unknown person who had sold the *Aubyn Letters*. The subject was one not likely to fix her attention – she was not a curious woman.

Glennard at this point laid down his fork and glanced at her between the candle-shades. The alternative explanation of her indifference was not slow in presenting itself. Her head had the same listening droop as when he had caught sight of her the day before in Flamel's company; the attitude revived the vividness of his impression. It was simple enough, after all. She had ceased to care for him because she cared for someone else.

As he followed her upstairs he felt a sudden stirring of his dormant anger. His sentiments had lost their artificial complexity. He had already acquitted her of any connivance in his baseness, and he felt only that he loved her and that she had escaped him. This was now, strangely enough, his dominant thought: the sense that he and she had passed through the fusion of love and had emerged from it as incommunicably apart as though the transmutation had never taken place. Every other passion, he mused, left some mark upon the nature; but love passed like the flight of a ship across the waters.

She dropped into her usual seat near the lamp, and he leant against the chimney, moving about with an inattentive hand the knick-knacks on the mantel.

Suddenly he caught sight of her reflection in the mirror. She was looking at him. He turned and their eyes met.

He moved across the room and stood before her.

'There's something that I want to say to you,' he began in a low tone.

She held his gaze, but her colour deepened. He noticed again, with a jealous pang, how her beauty had gained in warmth and meaning. It was as though a transparent cup had been filled with wine. He looked at her ironically.

'I've never prevented your seeing your friends here,' he broke out. 'Why do you meet Flamel in out-of-the-way places? Nothing makes a woman so cheap –'

She rose abruptly and they faced each other a few feet apart.

'What do you mean?' she asked.

'I saw you with him last Sunday on the Riverside Drive,' he went on, the utterance of the charge reviving his anger.

'Ah,' she murmured. She sank into her chair again and began to play with a paperknife that lay on the table at her elbow.

Her silence exasperated him.

'Well?' he burst out. 'Is that all you have to say?'

'Do you wish me to explain?' she asked, proudly.

'Do you imply I haven't the right to?'

'I imply nothing. I will tell you whatever you wish to know. I went for a walk with Mr Flamel because he asked me to.'

'I didn't suppose you went uninvited. But there are certain things a sensible woman doesn't do. She doesn't slink about in out-of-the-way streets with men. Why couldn't you have seen him here?'

She hesitated. 'Because he wanted to see me alone.'

'Did he, indeed? And may I ask if you gratify all his wishes with equal alacrity?'

'I don't know that he has any others where I am concerned.' She paused again and then continued, in a voice that somehow had an under-note of warning. 'He wished to bid me goodbye. He's going away.'

Glennard turned on her a startled glance. 'Going away?'

'He's going to Europe tomorrow. He goes for a long time. I supposed you knew.'

The last phrase revived his irritation. 'You forget that I depend on you for my information about Flamel. He's your friend and not mine. In fact, I've sometimes wondered at your going out of your way to be so civil to him when you must see plainly enough that I don't like him.'

Her answer to this was not immediate. She seemed to be choosing her words with care, not so much for her own sake as for his, and his exasperation was increased by the suspicion that she was trying to spare him.

'He was your friend before he was mine. I never knew him till I was married. It was you who brought him to the house and who seemed to wish me to like him.'

Glennard gave a short laugh. The defence was feebler than

he had expected: she was certainly not a clever woman.

'Your deference to my wishes is really beautiful; but it's not the first time in history that a man has made a mistake in introducing his friends to his wife. You must, at any rate, have seen since then that my enthusiasm had cooled; but so, perhaps, has your eagerness to oblige me.'

She met this with a silence that seemed to rob the taunt of half its efficacy.

'Is that what you imply?' he pressed her.

'No,' she answered with sudden directness. 'I noticed some time ago that you seemed to dislike him, but since then –'

'Well – since then?'

'I've imagined that you had reasons for still wishing me to be civil to him, as you call it.'

'Ah,' said Glennard, with an effort at lightness; but his irony dropped, for something in her voice made him feel that he and she stood at last in that naked desert of apprehension where meaning skulks vainly behind speech.

'And why did you imagine this?' The blood mounted to his forehead. 'Because he told you that I was under obligations to him?'

She turned pale. 'Under obligations?'

'Oh, don't let's beat about the bush. Didn't he tell you it was I who published Mrs Aubyn's letters? Answer me that.'

'No,' she said; and after a moment which seemed given to the weighing of alternatives, she added: 'No one told me.'

'You didn't know, then?'

She seemed to speak with an effort. 'Not until – not until –'

'Till I gave you those papers to sort?'

Her head sank.

'You understood then?'

'Yes.'

He looked at her immovable face. 'Had you suspected – before?' was slowly wrung from him.

'At times – yes –' Her voice dropped to a whisper.

'Why? From anything that was said –?'

There was a shade of pity in her glance. 'No one said anything – no one told me anything.' She looked away from him. 'It was your manner –'

'My manner?'

'Whenever the book was mentioned. Things you said – once or twice – your irritation – I can't explain.'

Glennard, unconsciously, had moved nearer. He breathed like a man who has been running. 'You knew, then, you knew –' he stammered. The avowal of her love for Flamel would have hurt him less, would have rendered her less remote. 'You knew – you knew –' he repeated; and suddenly his anguish gathered voice. 'My God!' he cried, 'you suspected it first, you say – and then you knew it – this damnable, this accursed thing; you knew it months ago – it's months since I put that paper in your way – and yet you've done nothing, you've said nothing, you've made no sign, you've lived alongside of me as if it had made no difference – no difference in either of our lives. What are you made of, I wonder? Don't you see the hideous ignominy of it? Don't you see how you've shared in my disgrace? Or haven't you any sense of shame?'

He preserved sufficient lucidity, as the words poured from him, to see how fatally they invited her derision; but something told him they had both passed beyond the phase of obvious retaliations, and that if any chord in her responded it would not be that of scorn.

He was right. She rose slowly and moved towards him.

'Haven't you had enough – without that?' she said, in a strange voice of pity.

He stared at her. 'Enough –?'

'Of misery…'

An iron band seemed loosened from his temples. 'You saw then?…' he whispered.

'Oh, God – oh, God –' she sobbed. She dropped beside him and hid her anguish against his knees. They clung thus in silence a long time, driven together down the same fierce blast of shame.

When at length she lifted her face he averted his. Her scorn would have hurt him less than the tears on his hands.

She spoke languidly, like a child emerging from a passion of weeping. 'It was for the money –?'

His lips shaped an assent.

'That was the inheritance – that we married on?'

'Yes.'

She drew back and rose to her feet. He sat watching her as she wandered away from him.

'You hate me,' broke from him.

She made no answer.

'Say you hate me!' he persisted.

'That would have been so simple,' she answered with a strange smile. She dropped into a chair near the writing table and rested a bowed forehead on her hand.

'Was it much –?' she began at length.

'Much –?' he returned, vaguely.

'The money.'

'The money?' That part of it seemed to count so little that for a moment he did not follow her thought.

'It must be paid back,' she insisted. 'Can you do it?'

'Oh, yes,' he returned, listlessly. 'I can do it.'

'I would make any sacrifice for that!' she urged.

He nodded. 'Of course.' He sat staring at her in dry-eyed

self-contempt. 'Do you count on its making much difference?'

'Much difference?'

'In the way I feel – or you feel about me?'

She shook her head.

'It's the least part of it,' he groaned.

'It's the only part we can repair.'

'Good heavens! If there were any reparation –' He rose quickly and crossed the space that divided them. 'Why did you never speak?'

'Haven't you answered that yourself?'

'Answered it?'

'Just now – when you told me you did it for me.'

She paused a moment and then went on with a deepening note – 'I would have spoken if I could have helped you.'

'But you must have despised me.'

'I've told you that would have been simpler.'

'But how could you go on like this – hating the money?'

'I knew you'd speak in time. I wanted you, first, to hate it as I did.'

He gazed at her with a kind of awe. 'You're wonderful,' he murmured. 'But you don't yet know the depths I've reached.'

She raised an entreating hand. 'I don't want to!'

'You're afraid, then, that you'll hate me?'

'No – but that you'll hate *me*. Let me understand without your telling me.'

'You can't. It's too base. I thought you didn't care because you loved Flamel.'

She blushed deeply. 'Don't – don't –' she warned him.

'I haven't the right to, you mean?'

'I mean that you'll be sorry.'

He stood imploringly before her. 'I want to say something worse – something more outrageous. If you don't understand *this* you'll be perfectly justified in ordering me out of the house.'

She answered him with a glance of divination. 'I shall understand – but you'll be sorry.'

'I must take my chance of that.' He moved away and tossed the books about the table. Then he swung round and faced her. 'Does Flamel care for you?' he asked.

Her flush deepened, but she still looked at him without anger. 'What would be the use?' she said, with a note of sadness.

'Ah, I didn't ask *that*,' he penitently murmured.

'Well, then –'

To this adjuration he made no response beyond that of gazing at her with an eye which seemed now to view her as a mere factor in an immense redistribution of meanings.

'I insulted Flamel today. I let him see that I suspected him of having told you. I hated him because he knew about the letters.'

He caught the spreading horror of her eyes, and for an instant he had to grapple with the new temptation they lit up. Then he said, with an effort, 'Don't blame him – he's impeccable. He helped me to get them published; but I lied to him too; I pretended they were written to another man… a man who was dead…'

She raised her arms in a gesture that seemed to ward off his blows.

'You *do* despise me!' he insisted.

'Ah, that poor woman – that poor woman –' he heard her murmur.

'I spare no one, you see!' he triumphed over her. She kept her face hidden.

'You do hate me, you do despise me!' he strangely exulted.

'Be silent!' she commanded him; but he seemed no longer conscious of any check on his gathering purpose.

'He cared for you – he cared for you,' he repeated, 'and he never told you of the letters –'

She sprang to her feet. 'How can you?' she flamed. 'How dare you? *That* –!'

Glennard was ashy pale. 'It's a weapon… like another…'

'A scoundrel's!'

He smiled wretchedly. 'I should have used it in his place.'

'Stephen! Stephen!' she cried, as though to drown the blasphemy on his lips. She swept to him with a rescuing gesture. 'Don't say such things. I forbid you! It degrades us both.'

He put her back with trembling hands. 'Nothing that I say of myself can degrade you. We're on different levels.'

'I'm on yours, wherever it is!'

He lifted his head and their gaze flowed together.

14

The great renewals take effect as imperceptibly as the first workings of spring. Glennard, though he felt himself brought nearer to his wife, was still, as it were, hardly within speaking distance. He was but laboriously acquiring the rudiments of a new language; and he had to grope for her through the dense fog of his humiliation, the distorting vapour against which his personality loomed grotesque and mean.

Only the fact that we are unaware how well our nearest know us enables us to live with them. Love is the most impregnable refuge of self-esteem, and we hate the eye that reaches to our nakedness. If Glennard did not hate his wife it was slowly, sufferingly, that there was born in him that profounder passion which made his earlier feeling seem a mere commotion of the blood. He was like a child coming back to the sense of an enveloping presence: her nearness was a breast on which he leaned.

They did not, at first, talk much together, and each beat a devious track about the outskirts of the subject that lay between them like a haunted wood. But every word, every action, seemed to glance at it, to draw towards it, as though a fount of healing sprang in its poisoned shade. If only they might cut away through the thicket to that restoring spring!

Glennard, watching his wife with the intentness of a wanderer to whom no natural sign is negligible, saw that she had taken temporary refuge in the purpose of renouncing the money. If both, theoretically, owned the inefficacy of such amends, the woman's instinctive subjectiveness made her find relief in this crude form of penance. Glennard saw that she meant to live as frugally as possible till what she deemed their debt was discharged; and he prayed she might not discover how far-reaching, in its merely material sense, was the obligation she thus hoped to acquit. Her mind was fixed on the sum originally paid for the letters, and this he knew he could lay aside in a year or two. He was touched, meanwhile, by the spirit that made her discard the petty luxuries which she regarded as the sign of their bondage. Their shared renunciations drew her nearer to him, helped, in their evidence of her helplessness, to restore the full protecting stature of his love. And still they did not speak.

It was several weeks later that, one afternoon by the drawing-room fire, she handed him a letter that she had been reading when he entered.

'I've heard from Mr Flamel,' she said.

It was as though a latent presence had suddenly become visible to both. Glennard took the letter mechanically.

'It's from Smyrna,' she said. 'Won't you read it?'

He handed it back. 'You can tell me about it – his hand's so illegible.' He wandered to the other end of the room and then turned and stood before her. 'I've been thinking of writing to Flamel,' he said.

She looked up.

'There's one point,' he continued, slowly, 'that I ought to clear up. I told him you'd known about the letters all along; for a long time, at least; and I saw how it hurt him. It was just what I meant to do, of course; but I can't leave him to that false impression; I must write him.'

She received this without outward movement, but he saw that the depths were stirred. At length she returned, in a hesitating tone, 'Why do you call it a false impression? I did know.'

'Yes, but I implied you didn't care.'

'Ah!'

He still stood looking down on her. 'Don't you want me to set that right?' he pursued.

She lifted her head and fixed him bravely. 'It isn't necessary,' she said.

Glennard flushed with the shock of the retort; then, with a gesture of comprehension, 'No,' he said, 'with you it couldn't be; but I might still set myself right.'

She looked at him gently. 'Don't I,' she murmured, 'do that?'

'In being yourself merely? Alas, the rehabilitation's too complete! You make me seem – to myself even – what I'm not; what I can never be. I can't, at times, defend myself from the delusion; but I can at least enlighten others.'

The flood was loosened, and kneeling by her he caught her hands. 'Don't you see that it's become an obsession with me? That if I could strip myself down to the last lie – only there'd always be another one left under it! – and do penance naked in the marketplace, I should at least have the relief of easing one anguish by another? Don't you see that the worst of my torture is the impossibility of such amends?'

Her hands lay in his without returning pressure. 'Ah, poor woman, poor woman,' he heard her sigh.

'Don't pity her, pity me! What have I done to her or to you, after all? You're both inaccessible! It was myself I sold.'

He took an abrupt turn away from her; then halted before her again. 'How much longer,' he burst out, 'do you suppose you can stand it? You've been magnificent, you've been inspired, but what's the use? You can't wipe out the ignominy of it. It's miserable for you and it does *her* no good!'

She lifted a vivid face. 'That's the thought I can't bear!' she cried.

'What thought?'

'That it does her no good – all you're feeling, all you're suffering. Can it be that it makes no difference?'

He avoided her challenging glance. 'What's done is done,' he muttered.

'Is it ever, quite, I wonder?' she mused. He made no answer and they lapsed into one of the pauses that are a subterranean channel of communication.

It was she who, after a while, began to speak, with a new suffusing diffidence that made him turn a roused eye on her.

'Don't they say,' she asked, feeling her way as in a kind of tender apprehensiveness, 'that the early Christians, instead of pulling down the heathen temples – the temples of the unclean gods – purified them by turning them to their own uses? I've always thought one might do that with one's actions – the actions one loathes but can't undo. One can make, I mean, a wrong the door to other wrongs or an impassable wall against them…' Her voice wavered on the word. 'We can't always tear down the temples we've built to the unclean gods, but we can put good spirits in the house of evil – the spirits of mercy and shame and understanding, that might never have come to us if we hadn't been in such great need…'

She moved over to him and laid a hand on his. His head was bent and he did not change his attitude. She sat down beside him without speaking; but their silences now were fertile as rain clouds – they quickened the seeds of understanding.

At length he looked up. 'I don't know,' he said, 'what spirits have come to live in the house of evil that I built – but you're there and that's enough. It's strange,' he went on after another pause, 'she wished the best for me so often, and now, at last, it's through her that it's come to me. But for her I shouldn't have known you – it's through her that I've found you. Sometimes – do you know? – that makes it hardest – makes me most intolerable to myself. Can't you see that it's the worst thing I've got to face? I sometimes think I could have borne it better if you hadn't understood! I took everything from her – everything – even to the poor shelter of loyalty she'd trusted in – the only thing I *could* have left her! – I took everything from her, I deceived her, I despoiled her, I destroyed her – and she's given me *you* in return!'

His wife's cry caught him up. 'It isn't that she's given *me* to you – it is that she's given you to yourself.' She leaned to him as though swept forward on a wave of pity. 'Don't you see,' she went on, as his eyes hung on her, 'that that's the gift you can't escape from, the debt you're pledged to acquit? Don't you see that you've never before been what she thought you, and that now, so wonderfully, she's made you into the man she loved? *That's* worth suffering for, worth dying for, to a woman – that's the gift she would have wished to give!'

'Ah,' he cried, 'but woe to him by whom it cometh. What did I ever give her?'

'The happiness of giving,' she said.

NOTES

1. Horace Walpole (1717–97) is considered one of literature's greatest epistolers, with his letters providing invaluable portraits of Georgian England.

2. Hannah More (1745–1833) was a leading member of the Blue Stocking Circle and a lively letter-writer; Harriet Martineau (1802–76) was a campaigner for free trade and women's rights and also a tireless letter-writer.

3. Peter Abelard (1079–1142) and his tragic love for Héloïse formed the basis for Alexander Pope's heroic epistle, 'Eloisa to Abelard' (1717).

4. Prosper Mérimée (1803–70) was involved in a passionate love affair with Emilie Lacoste which resulted in a duel between her husband and the poet.

5. French novelist George Sand (1804–76) had a series of high-profile affairs, including one with Gustave Flaubert (1821–80), and the lovers exchanged numerous letters.

6. Charlotte Elisabeth Aïssé (1694–1733) is remembered for her correspondence with Madame Calandrinil and her lively portraits of French society life. The Comtesse de Sabran exchanged numerous letters with the Chevalier de Boufflers (1738–1815) during his final years as Governor of Senegal (1778–88); these were subsequently published in 1875.

7. Percy Bysshe Shelley (1792–1822) eloped with Harriet Westbrook (1795–1816) when she was only sixteen, but the marriage later collapsed and, in 1816, she drowned herself in the Serpentine river.

BIOGRAPHICAL NOTE

Edith Wharton (née Newbold Jones) was born in 1862 into a wealthy New York family. She was educated privately in New York and Europe, and in 1885 she married Edward Robbins Wharton, a banker from Boston. They settled in France in 1907 but the marriage was a troubled one, and they eventually divorced in 1913, due partly to Edward's mental ill heath, and partly to Edith's struggles to balance the duties of a wife with her ambitions as a writer. She had published her first book, *The Decoration of Houses* in 1897.

After her divorce, Edith continued to live in France, where she would remain until her death. She took on the role of 'literary hostess' and her Paris home saw frequent visits from Henry James, Walter Berry and a number of other writers. She herself had gained a considerable reputation as a writer with a number of books behind her: *The Greater Inclination* had appeared in 1899, followed by *The Touchstone* (1900), and, in 1905, *The House of Mirth*. France provided the setting for a number of her novels, *Madame de Treymes* (1907) and *The Reef* (1912) among them.

During the First World War she worked for various American newspapers, and became involved in work with refugees. She continued to write novels and in 1920 produced perhaps her most famous novel, *The Age of Innocence* which went on to win the Pulitzer Prize. This study of New-York society life brilliantly encapsulated many of her themes and concerns as a writer. These, and in particular the role of women in turn-of-the-century America, she also explored in her numerous short stories.

She was still working on her final novel, *The Buccaneers*, when she died on 11th August 1937.

HESPERUS PRESS – 100 PAGES

Hesperus Press, as suggested by the Latin motto, is committed to bringing near what is far – far both in space and time. Works written by the greatest authors, and unjustly neglected or simply little known in the English-speaking world, are made accessible through new translations and a completely fresh editorial approach. Through these short classic works, each around 100 pages in length, the reader will be introduced to the greatest writers from all times and all cultures.

For more information on Hesperus Press, please visit our website: **www.hesperuspress.com**

SELECTED TITLES FROM HESPERUS PRESS

Author	Title	Foreword writer
Pietro Aretino	The School of Whoredom	Paul Bailey
Jane Austen	Love and Friendship	Fay Weldon
Honoré de Balzac	Colonel Chabert	A.N. Wilson
Charles Baudelaire	On Wine and Hashish	Margaret Drabble
Giovanni Boccaccio	Life of Dante	A.N. Wilson
Charlotte Brontë	The Green Dwarf	Libby Purves
Mikhail Bulgakov	The Fatal Eggs	Doris Lessing
Giacomo Casanova	The Duel	Tim Parks
Miguel de Cervantes	The Dialogue of the Dogs	
Anton Chekhov	The Story of a Nobody	Louis de Bernières
Wilkie Collins	Who Killed Zebedee?	Martin Jarvis
Arthur Conan Doyle	The Tragedy of the Korosko	Tony Robinson

Niccolò Machiavelli	*Life of Castruccio Castracani*	Richard Overy
Katherine Mansfield	*In a German Pension*	Linda Grant
Guy de Maupassant	*Butterball*	Germaine Greer
Herman Melville	*The Enchanted Isles*	Margaret Drabble
Francis Petrarch	*My Secret Book*	Germaine Greer
Luigi Pirandello	*Loveless Love*	
Edgar Allan Poe	*Eureka*	Sir Patrick Moore
Alexander Pope	*Scriblerus*	Peter Ackroyd
Alexander Pushkin	*Dubrovsky*	Patrick Neate
François Rabelais	*Gargantua*	Paul Bailey
François Rabelais	*Pantagruel*	Paul Bailey
Friedrich von Schiller	*The Ghost-seer*	Martin Jarvis
Percy Bysshe Shelley	*Zastrozzi*	Germaine Greer
Stendhal	*Memoirs of an Egotist*	Doris Lessing
Robert Louis Stevenson	*Dr Jekyll and Mr Hyde*	Helen Dunmore
Theodor Storm	*The Lake of the Bees*	Alan Sillitoe
Italo Svevo	*A Perfect Hoax*	Tim Parks
Jonathan Swift	*Directions to Servants*	Colm Tóibín
W.M. Thackeray	*Rebecca and Rowena*	Matthew Sweet
Leo Tolstoy	*Hadji Murat*	Colm Tóibín
Ivan Turgenev	*Faust*	Simon Callow
Mark Twain	*The Diary of Adam and Eve*	John Updike
Giovanni Verga	*Life in the Country*	Paul Bailey
Jules Verne	*A Fantasy of Dr Ox*	Gilbert Adair
Oscar Wilde	*The Portrait of Mr W.H.*	Peter Ackroyd
Virginia Woolf	*Carlyle's House and Other Sketches*	Doris Lessing
Virginia Woolf	*Monday or Tuesday*	Scarlett Thomas
Emile Zola	*For a Night of Love*	A.N. Wilson